TRACKER'S CANYON

TRACKER'S CANYON

PAM WITHERS

DUNDURN
TORONTO

Image credits: istock.com/da-kuk
Printer: Webcom

Library and Archives Canada Cataloguing in Publication

Withers, Pam, author
    Tracker's canyon / Pam Withers.

Issued also in electronic formats.
ISBN 978-1-4597-3963-5 (softcover).--ISBN 978-1-4597-3964-2
(PDF).--ISBN 978-1-4597-3965-9 (EPUB)

    I. Title.

PS8595.I8453T73 2017   jC813'.6   C2016-908133-8
                                                C2016-908134-6

1   2   3   4   5   21   20   19   18   17

Conseil des Arts du Canada Canada Council for the Arts Canadä ONTARIO ARTS COUNCIL CONSEIL DES ARTS DE L'ONTARIO an Ontario government agency un organisme du gouvernement de l'Ontario

We acknowledge the support of the **Canada Council for the Arts**, which last year invested $153 million to bring the arts to Canadians throughout the country, and the **Ontario Arts Council** for our publishing program. We also acknowledge the financial support of the **Government of Ontario**, through the **Ontario Book Publishing Tax Credit** and the **Ontario Media Development Corporation**, and the **Government of Canada**.

Nous remercions le **Conseil des arts du Canada** de son soutien. L'an dernier, le Conseil a investi 153 millions de dollars pour mettre de l'art dans la vie des Canadiennes et des Canadiens de tout le pays.

Printed and bound in Canada.

VISIT US AT

 dundurn.com | @dundurnpress | dundurnpress | dundurnpress

Dundurn
3 Church Street, Suite 500
Toronto, Ontario, Canada
M5E 1M2

For Alix Jane de Ruydts

CHAPTER 1

Bare feet are soundless. Combined with stealth, they can buy a sliver of freedom. A daily sliver of freedom is all I need, but I need it like oxygen. Seriously.

So, being the Sultan of Stealth, I sneak out of my bedroom before dawn and pad ninja-like down the hallway.

First I peer into my mother's room, where the weak glow of her bedside clock identifies her shape, shrouded by twisted sheets. A hand dangles beside the nightstand, crowded with pill bottles.

I sigh, then catch myself. I've sworn off sad and don't do "down" anymore. Instead, I remind myself to take comfort in the gentle rise and fall of her chest.

Hang in there, Mom. And forgive me, but I've got to get a breath of fresh air. I move away from her like a shadow down the worn stair treads. My nose scrunches up as it passes the unwashed dishes in the sink; my bare feet expertly negotiate the greasy kitchen floor.

I know just how to open the back door without its rusty hinges squealing. Oiling them is somewhere on my to-do list. But the dishes and scrubbing the kitchen floor are higher priority — as in, I've got to check off these new Head of the Household duties in between this jailbreak and the high school's morning bell.

Like a fake sumo wrestler who bounces trouble off his cool rubber suit, I'm finding the chunk of chores and attempt at a new attitude easier every week. If Mom were more with it, she'd be proud of me. If Dad hadn't disappeared — well, then I wouldn't need the rubber suit *or* have to face these new obligations. But yeah, he'd be proud of me, too.

If only a raise came with the promotion.

I jog barefoot down the forest trail, pine cones cushioning my calluses, early birdsong filling my ears, first sunrays lighting up the corrugated trunks of cedar trees. I like to go barefoot 'cause it puts my feet in closer touch with the ground.

Soon it's time to pause and let my old self come out and play. I become the skilled tracker my father helped me become. *Guilt, get lost for now!*

Some guys pursue fame. Some chase girls. I stalk animals. Not to hurt them, of course. Trackers just track. So I stop and crouch in the dewy grass, breathe in the forest, and funnel all my senses into finding a creature to follow. Small hoofprints — *bingo!* Soon I'm trailing a mother deer and two fawns.

The size, distance between the tracks, and how clear the imprint is help me calculate how far ahead the deer are and how fast they're moving. Perfect: I'll sight them and be home before Mom wakes up.

Within twenty minutes, salal bushes are scratching my thighs and flies are haloing my head, but patience being my specialty, I don't move an inch. *Yes! There they are.* For five sweet minutes, happiness flows through me just watching two spotted fawns prance about the meadow, under the watchful almond eyes of their mother.

As they munch the spring grass, I mentally brush my fingers against the warmth of the smaller fawn's smooth, brown neck.

Embrace calm, my father always urged. *Slow down, clear your mind, make yourself invisible.*

Waiting for the right second to move, I ignore the tickle of ants crawling up my leg, the sting of mosquitoes feeding on my neck, the sweat trickling down my back. A breeze whispers through the trees, a faraway frog croaks, a fleeing chickadee scolds. Nature is like a drug to me. Being outdoors, smelling and hearing everything close-up, and challenging my senses: it's the best high ever.

I scan past the meadow to the wash of orange-yellow brightening the horizon and glance left, right, and down, just like Dad taught me. *Damn.* The prick of pain that comes with any memory of him distracts me just long enough that I fail to notice the forest going quiet. Very quiet.

Too late, the mother deer's head lifts and stiffens; her tail quivers. Then, with only the slightest of creaks from a branch a few trees behind me, a blur of gold arcs through the air, takes two bounds, and lands on the smallest fawn.

Holy crap. Mother and surviving fawn bolt. The cougar's teeth sink into the fawn's neck — the neck I'd been imagining stroking. I choke off a cry.

"Hey!" The shout from behind makes me jump.

As the cougar drags his prey to the edge of the meadow, boots pound toward me. Before I can spin around, two firm hands lock on my shoulders and haul me back.

"Kid, what do you think you are playing at? That cougar could have just as easily jumped *you!*" A European accent.

I shake myself free, turn, square my shoulders, and eye this tall stranger in camouflage clothes. *Who does he think he is, attempting to lecture a near guru of this terrain?* He's no more than twenty-five years old, I decide. He has short curly brown hair and a thin moustache on his not-unfriendly face.

· "I'm not a kid," I declare with my hands on my hips.

"No?" He half smiles. "What are you — like, fifteen?"

The interloper is tall and as solid as a middle-weight champ. My gut says the guy's okay. Still, I judge it best to be polite but firm.

"Sixteen." I level my eyes at him. "And you just ruined everything. I've been tracking those deer for half an hour." I look toward the meadow; the cougar has disappeared with its catch. I turn back.

The man leans against a tree with a smirk. "Oh, so you think you are a tracker, do you? Not such a great one, if you did not notice the cougar or me, kid. Classic case of the hunter becoming the hunted."

"Well, I guess I must be pretty special to have two hunters following me."

His smile widens. "I was tracking the cat when I saw you trying to follow the deer. Figured I had better speed up, in case the cougar updated his breakfast plans."

I relax a little. "Whatever. Thanks, I guess."

"You are welcome. Your parents know where you are?"

I shift my bare feet in the dirt and study the last hoofprints of the unlucky fawn. "I don't have parents."

"No parents, huh?" He smothers a laugh. "So, let me guess. You live on your own in a cave near here, and you skin and eat any deer the cougar does not get? A real wannabe Indian tracker!"

"Better than someone who tracks trackers," I say evenly. "Tristan Gordon," I add, extending my hand.

"Dominik Goralski," he responds, crushing my palm in his. "I did not mean to offend you. You actually did pretty well tracking that deer for a guy your age."

"You think?" I pause, then ask, "Do you live around here?"

"I do Search and Rescue work in Poland; I'm here on vacation. Let me give you a tip or two. First, never focus on just one thing. You should be working on sensing an animal, even if it is downwind. Second, when I saw you scanning the horizon back there, you looked left, right, and down. Exactly like you should have. You just forgot to look up, too."

I bristle at some stranger telling me how to track, but damn, the guy's sharp. *How many times did I hear that from my dad?* "Yeah. Good advice. My weak point, I've been told," I admit.

"Look up now, and tell me what you see."

I lift my face and watch a flock of slender birds with long, pointed wings, hunting insects in the air. "Swallows."

"Good. And where are they headed?"

"West, *duh*."

"No, I mean where, exactly? I am not from around here."

My chest tightens. Where are they headed? Worst question he could ask. "Swallow Canyon."

"Ah, the famous Swallow Canyon. You have been there?"

I purse my lips to seal all emo inside. "Yes."

Something gives me away. His eyes are clamped on me like he's going to unlock my secret.

"Sorry. I've got to go," I say hurriedly. "I've got a mountain of chores to do before school. But enjoy your time in British Columbia, and I appreciate the tracking tips."

"Okay, Tristan, see you around. Stay safe."

As my feet turn homeward and speed up, I wonder if I'll see the guy again. I forgot to ask how long he'd be around. Oh well. When I lift my head for a second, I see that the swallows, like my dad, have disappeared.

CHAPTER 2

"Tristan, my man. A rare sighting! Where've you been lately?"

I pause as I'm locking my bike to the school rack and slap my friend lightly on the back. "Nowhere, Phil. What's happening?"

"Nothing much." He shifts his mud-spattered backpack and punches me back. "When're you going to show your mug at climbing club, eh? It's been forever."

I chuckle and look away. "Soon. Hey, I'm giving the other guys a chance with the girls in the club."

"As if. Last time I saw you, you said the girls are too into mothering you since — uh, how *is* your mom?"

"She's great," I say, feeling my mouth press into a tight line.

"Awesome! It's been eight months, after all." He's studying me closely despite my upbeat tone.

"Minus two weeks," I correct him.

"Okay. I'm so hyped you're finally coming back. When? Can't wait to tell the guys."

"Any day," I lie. No way can I tell him about the lack of cash for club fees and the shortage of hours in the day, thanks to chores. *I don't mind this more restricted life,* I try to tell myself, *because nothing matters more than helping Mom right now.* But hell if I'm going to let anyone know what's really up in the Gordon household.

"It's been boring on the climbing wall without you," he continues as we move into the school.

"No doubt." I smile. "Except for the new kid, Dean. Mini Spider-Man." The last time I showed up at the club was two months ago, the same day as a brand-new kid in town asked to join. I still recall the boy's natural talent and have seen him around once or twice since. "Who'd have thought a twelve-year-old could climb like that? Or that we'd ever let a seventh grader into the club?"

Phil shrugs. "Only 'cause you suggested it that first day he showed. I admit he's amazing. I've actually learned a few moves from him. But you were the star, man. We need you back."

"*Were*, eh! Guess I'd better get my ass back in there."

The bell sounds. We hurry to our lockers, grab our books, and slam the locker doors shut.

"Later, man," Phil says as he heads up the hall to class.

"Later," I say. Books in arms, I wait till Phil has gone before I press my forehead against the cool steel of my locker. I miss climbing club and my friends so much it hurts. But I must not think about it. I count to five till the funk disappears. Then, shoulders back and head held high, I breathe deeply and wade through the crowds to class.

• • •

An hour into Math, students point out the window.

"Class!" snaps Mr. Winters, to no effect.

A fire truck wails up the main street of our little town (population two thousand), its flashing red lights bouncing off the school's football field posts, where it stops. I leap up to join the students crowding the window; even Mr. Winters stands there gawking. One look and I'm out of the classroom, through the main school doors, and onto the football field, sprinting over its sweet-smelling, fresh-mown grass.

Our school, edged by evergreens, has a bunch of tall Douglas firs beside the playing field, one of them maybe eighty feet high. Mini Spider-Man — Dean the amazing climber kid — has somehow managed to climb three-quarters of the way to the top of that one.

"Don't move!" Principal Tolmie calls up to him.

Teachers and a ton of kids have circled the tree. Every panicked voice has a different set of instructions.

"Don't look down!"

"Hold tight!"

"Wait for the firefighters!"

There's a shrill whine as the fire truck lifts its mechanical ladder to the branch where the boy with bushy black hair sits. He's smiling and as calm as a Buddha statue.

Way to go, Dean, I think, half proud of my former club mate, even though I hardly know him. *Except you're going to be in a shitload of trouble.* I do a fast assessment of the tree trunk between the ground and the boy, ready to climb up and coach him down if needed.

Then a mountain bike catches my eye — someone wheeling at gravel-spitting speed toward the school. The bike clatters to the pavement, and a tall, thin woman maybe twenty years old and wearing black fitness gear strides to the tree, lifts her head, and shades her eyes.

"Dean!" she shouts matter-of-factly, like she has seen it a thousand times before.

Dean actually smiles down at her, pulls a stick of black licorice from his shorts pocket, and starts chewing on it. *She's barely old enough to be out of high school herself,* I think. *Babysitter? Sister?*

She tosses her long, black hair over her shoulders and marches toward the fire truck, all business-like. I edge closer.

"I suggest you retract the ladder … safer if he climbs down on his own."

Some nerve, telling the fire department what to do.

To my amazement, a firefighter reverses the truck ladder, and the woman in black strolls to the base of the tree.

"So sorry," she apologizes along the way to the teachers and principal, then signals Dean.

He nods, pockets his licorice, and down-climbs, never hesitating, never faltering, like the closest relative to a monkey I've seen. I'm tempted to burst out cheering.

On the ground, before the principal reaches them, the young woman embraces the boy and he hugs her back fiercely. Like, way too tightly for a twelve-year-old with half the school staring at him.

Then she grips his shoulders, puts her forehead against his, and delivers some kind of quiet lecture. He just nods, blinks, and glances up at Principal Tolmie, who is headed their way looking like a police officer itching to clamp handcuffs on someone.

"All yours." The woman hands Dean over and takes her time striding back to her bike, thanking the firefighters on the way.

Seriously? So this sister or whatever she is just arrives, takes over, orders him down, then leaves? No, not yet, as it turns out. What she does next will haunt me for hours. She picks up her bike, turns, and glares at me. A long, slow, vicious look. I turn to see if there's someone behind me, maybe some enemy she has bad blood with.

I've never seen the woman before, so there's clearly some mistake. It's only as she turns to ride off — tires spewing gravel, once again — that I catch the logo on her T-shirt. It sends shivers through my body: *Swallow Canyon Expeditions.*

• • •

Spring means the days are getting warmer and longer. By the time I've biked home from the supermarket and drugstore, I'm imagining pulling the dented barbeque out of our garage and grilling Mom a hamburger. Maybe it's red meat she needs. Or just a reason to come downstairs and sit on the back patio with me.

Later we could watch the stars come out and discuss which constellations are which, like the three of us used to do. Dad would have his stargazing chart laid out on the picnic table and his garage-sale telescope set up on a rickety tripod. He'd sit back on the wood bench he and I built, wearing that worn green sweater Mom knit him, a grin on his face and an arm around each of us. I swallow hard, remembering the clean, damp-wool smell and prickliness of his sweater when he hugged me.

When I see her bedroom window is open, curtains flapping in the breeze, my heart lifts. Then I spot Elspeth's moped by the back door, and my mood does a crash landing. *What's the witch up to now? She should've gone home an hour ago.*

I heave my backpack onto the linoleum kitchen counter and frown at the dirty dishes piled in the sink. Elspeth is happy to eat our food while fixing lunch for Mom — but do dishes? Not.

Never mind; she's too busy looking after Mom, and I'm the official dishes guy, it seems.

Something smells weird. *Lavender?*

"Tristan, honey. So glad you're home. Your mother's sleeping, but I stayed late so you and I could talk."

Talk? I glance at the new hair colour: pink. It clashes with her rainbow smock, purple miniskirt, and red clogs, but it brightens up the place, for sure. Where my uncle found this thirty-year-old space cadet and why Mom has fallen under Elspeth's spell is beyond me. *Oops. My negatory detect-o-meter is beeping.*

"Hi, Elspeth. Interesting hair colour. Hey, am I imagining it, or is there a fascinating fragrance in the air?"

"Lavender, darling. It's part of our aromatherapy session. It calms her."

"Cool. But is it possible she doesn't need to be calmed? Maybe she needs to get up and move, instead."

Elspeth reaches out to pat my hand; I slide it away and begin storing groceries. Aromatherapy, hypnotherapy, horoscope-reading, crystal-touching: these are what my uncle's paying for out of what I think should go toward groceries, repair bills — and my climbing club fees. But Elspeth is Mom's caretaker for now. And who knows? If she ever convinces me aromatherapy can make Mom better, I'll be the first to haul wheelbarrows of lavender home.

"So, Tristan, you know your mother is not mending with time as much as we hoped."

"Mmm."

"I feel she is drifting away from us."

I picture a lily pad floating across a lake, buffeted by wind, its brown edges curled down into the murky water.

"Tristan?"

"Yes."

Elspeth looks across our small living room and its few pieces of worn but sturdy furniture at the stairs, as if my mother might come gliding down in her nightgown any second and overhear us. She motions us into the living room, where I evict a basket of dirty laundry from the sofa so we can plunk down. With springs well-worn, the sofa sinks under our combined weight. She plays with the dozen or so rings on long, white fingers adorned by fake fingernails painted a startling pink.

I instruct myself to listen politely.

"When a loved one passes away and there's no body to grieve over," she begins, "the family's recovery process is prolonged, delayed."

"Uh-huh," I say, gritting my teeth, but only gently.

"Not so much in your case, dear," she adds with a lame pat on my shoulder that makes me recoil. "You are strong, and your need to be your mother's pillar has brought you through the worst already, which I admire."

Oh yeah? She thinks she's a psychic now?

"But with no … body," she continues, "there needs to be a special object that will draw out your mother's grief. Not the few things Search and Rescue returned. Something else, something special. You're okay with talking about this, right? I believe it's therapeutic. But I don't want to traumatize you, honey."

"I'm fine," I say, fingernails pressing into my palms, but only lightly.

She does a big, dramatic sigh. "Good. Because I feel she needs something important of his to hold on to, something that proves he's gone. It will help her in her recovery."

"But —" *How is this any of Elspeth's business? Why doesn't everyone just accept Dad is dead? Why do we have to talk about it?* I swallow a fat lump in my throat.

"Darling, I know we can't ever expect to find the body. But before he disappeared, he may have shed or dropped something Search and Rescue didn't find.

On a tree branch or ledge, perhaps. I feel it; I sense it. My extrasensory perception tells me this. And — well, you're a tracker and a canyoneer. And I know you want her to get better. If you could just try —"

"Search and Rescue tried for two whole weeks," I remind her. "And brought back his shredded sleeping bag and a few clothes."

"*Shh*, you'll wake her." Elspeth presses one of her pink-tipped fingernails to her lips. "Yes, Search and Rescue tried to find him alive, then tried to find the body. But their failure doesn't mean that you — the one with the true spiritual family connection — can't locate something they failed to discover. You're his son, Tristan. You have powers they don't."

I open my mouth, but when nothing comes out, I shut it again.

"I feel it in my bones, Tristan. Your ability to locate something else he left behind, darling. She'll come out of this depression. You'll be a family again."

"Tristan?" A sleepy voice drifts down from upstairs.

"Go, honey," Elspeth urges. She squeezes my hand. "Be gentle with her. We all need to gift her with our utmost patience for now. Then, when you return with what your father left behind for you, it will all be okay."

Elspeth, I decide, is crazier than bat shit. One pink hair short of wigged out. *Get me out of here.*

As I bolt up the stairs, I hear Elspeth heading out the door. In minutes, the putt-putt of her moped fades down the gravel road.

"Mom?"

She's propped up on her pillows, all bones and pale skin. I breathe in the reek of lavender. *What would Dad make of what she has become?* If he had known what it would do to her, he'd never have gone into Swallow Canyon that day.

"Can you close the window, Tristan? It's chilling me."

"Sure, Mom. How are you today?"

She shrugs and offers a wan smile. "Did you get my pills from the drugstore?"

"Yes."

She smoothes the old, shabby quilt that smells like it should've been washed three loads ago. I perch there and take her hand, my throat catching.

"Elspeth says you washed the dishes and mopped the floor this morning, but forgot to fix the kettle. She had to boil water in a pot to serve me some special herbal tea."

"Poor, poor Elspeth."

"I know you're not fond of her, Tristan, but she has been so helpful since — since our tragedy." Her voice is pleading. "I don't know what I'd do without her."

Her gaze drifts toward the closed window; she's on the edge of crying, as usual. *But it no longer rips me up*, I remind myself. *No more feeling small and helpless and useless. I have moved on — and filled my father's shoes pretty well, haven't I?* Someone had to.

So why does Mom just lie here, numb and wasting away?

No body to grieve over. Recovery process delayed.

"I got food today, Mom, but the money tin is empty now."

She nods vaguely. "Ask your uncle, darling. You're a good boy. Any luck with the washing machine?"

"Only if the goal was to drown the mouse population in the basement. I mopped up the mess and tried duct-taping the hose, but it didn't work. No worries — I'll ask Uncle Ted."

She smoothes my hair. "What will you make for dinner?"

"Lobster mornay? Just kidding. Hamburgers?"

She shakes her head. "Something lighter."

"Okay, the usual."

She smiles blandly. "Sounds good. Scrambled eggs."

"Can I get you a magazine or something? Or read to you from my joke book?"

"Thanks, Tristan, but I'm feeling rather sleepy."

"Maybe a little walk would wake you up? It's a nice day, Mom. We could go sit in the grotto." The grotto is a cool fake cave Dad and I built by the stream at the foot of our property. It's where we used to spend lots of fun family time.

Oops, mistake. The tears start down her cheeks.

… patience for now. Then, when you return with what your father left behind for you, it will all be okay.

"No!" I say out loud.

My mother's body jerks in alarm. "Tristan?"

"Sorry, Mom. Sorry, sorry." I lean across the bed and wrap her in my arms, absorb her sobs. *The more I absorb, the better she'll get, right?*

If only her shrivelled body didn't feel like a clutch of bones. Soon I leap up and run down the stairs, two at a time. I snatch the eggs and crack them so hard against the mixing bowl rim that the shells disintegrate into a thousand sticky pieces.

Embrace calm.

The bowl, suddenly gone blurry through my tears, is the one in which Mom, a former bakery manager, used to make brownies, cookies, and cakes, including special birthday cakes for me resembling things like fire engines, and later, anime action figures. And giant chocolate-coloured hearts for my dad. We were a real family then.

Maybe flinging pans around will drown out the memory of Elspeth's words.

"She — will — get — better," I declare to the moped tracks still visible out the kitchen window. "With or without your psycho-shit."

My negatory detect-o-meter is screeching. But at this moment, I don't have the energy to care.

CHAPTER 3

I roll up to the shop, lock my bike, and banish the guilt trip that hitched a ride over with me. I really hate asking my uncle for money.

"Hey, Uncle Ted." My mother's kind but ever-anxious brother, dressed in jeans and a wrinkled flannel shirt, is hunched over accounting books in the backroom, as usual.

"Tristan! Good to see you."

Except that he knows why I'm here. He knows it rips me up to come into the shop for any other reason.

"Mom says hi and to remind you about picking her up for the doctor's appointment."

"Hey, have I missed one yet? How's she doing?" He says it mechanically, like he doesn't really expect an answer.

I paste on a smile. "I don't like to bug you, Uncle Ted, but we're —"

"— out of grocery money already?" He wipes beads of sweat from his balding head and frowns at the columns of numbers in front of him.

"And one of the hoses to the washing machine thinks it's a fountain. I tried to fix it, but we might need a plumber."

"A plumber." The frown deepens.

"Sorry, Uncle Ted. I'm working on being a washer repair whiz, but I'm not there yet."

He leans back in the leather swivel chair, which squeaks just like it always did when my dad sat in it. I tamp down the longing for my father to step in, slap Uncle Ted on the back, muss up my hair, and tell us how business is booming and all is right with the world, even though things weren't great the months before he disappeared. We were struggling when it came to money, for sure. But he was Mr. Positive, Mr. Happy, Best Dad Ever.

Except for when he closed himself off in his study to read all those dusty books about the gold-rush days or spent hours at our creek with his gold pan.

"Time-warped 49er," the neighbours used to joke.

"My precious prospector," Mom teased him.

But everyone needs a hobby, and I loved the gold-rush stories he told, and the musical chime of flowing water when I joined him by the creek. I miss him, every piece of him. Just imagining his presence now warms the room.

"Trouble is, Tristan, the shop isn't doing so well," Uncle Ted is saying. "I just can't keep up with the business like your father did. It's him the customers came for, not me. And even he was finding it a challenge to turn a profit. I'm useless with accounting stuff. Plus, there's all the fuss with the insurance companies not having proof of his — what I'm saying is, I'm doing the best I can, but — oh, darn. I don't mean to trouble you when you and my sister have difficulties enough."

He produces his wallet, fishes out most of his bills, and lays them in my palm. "I'll call for a plumber, okay? How's school and stuff?"

My fingers close over the money. "School's excellent. I miss all my friends in climbing club, though. You know, if you cut back on Elspeth's hours —"

"Tristan, we've been through this before. She's Mary's biggest comfort, and — well, you're right, she costs a little, but not that much. Let's just wait till your mother is a little better." He lifts a hand and puts it awkwardly on my shoulder.

He seems to have missed the hint about climbing club fees, but — I sigh — he's right about Elspeth being important to Mom.

"Tristan," he says, "the coffee maker is on the fritz today. Any chance you could run down to the café and get me a decent cup of coffee? Grab yourself a doughnut while you're at it, and come back and sit with me a while."

"Sure, Uncle Ted." My taste buds are already wrapped around that doughnut.

• • •

Ten minutes later I'm about to re-enter the shop when I notice he has a customer, and she's wearing black fitness gear. I sink down on the wood bench outside the open window, hoping to learn more about the young woman I saw at school.

"I see," Uncle Ted is saying. "Well, unfortunately, it's Rafael you should talk with. He's the employee who can best advise you on canyoneering gear, but he's on vacation this week."

"So you're the owner?" she asks. "But you're not a climber or a canyoneer?"

Uncle Ted hangs his head. "I took over from my brother-in-law eight months ago. I don't know these sports like he did. Just holding down the fort till — Are you in a hurry for the equipment?"

"Well, yes, actually. Just had a couple of people book a trip on Sunday. It would be on Swallow Canyon Expeditions' account. I'm a new guide there. Name is Brigit Dowling. Here's my business card."

"Dowling, eh? You look young to be a guide," Uncle Ted says with a half smile.

"I'm nineteen and fully qualified," she replies briskly.

Dowling is Dean's last name, so she must be his sister, I reflect, before rising from my bench, strolling in, and handing the coffee — before it gets cold — to Uncle Ted.

"Dowling … " Uncle Ted repeats, scratching his head like maybe her name rings a bell with him. Then he shrugs like he has given up trying to place her.

"Welcome to Canyons and Trails. I'm Tristan Gordon. Can I help you?" I address this skinny woman with long, limp hair and a rather severe face.

She looks me up and down. "I don't know. Can you?"

"I'm betting I can. What kind of equipment are you after?"

"Anchors."

"Okay, what level of canyoneering will your customers be tackling? And are you thinking natural anchors or bolted belay stations?"

She pauses, looks from Uncle Ted to me. She's not good-looking, I decide, but has plenty of muscle tone and a self-assured manner.

"You're in good hands with my nephew," my uncle encourages her. "Hoping to get him to take over the shop soon."

I throw him the usual sardonic look. Uncle Ted needs to hold it together another year until I graduate, then go back to being a car mechanic. He pats me on my shoulder and lopes back to the rear office.

"We're intending to use boulder pinches for anchors," Brigit says.

I smile inwardly, knowing she's testing me.

"Then I'd suggest you go for sixteen-millimetre tubular webbing."

"And why's that?"

"Because it's stronger — better for making the knot chock anchors you'll probably set."

She nods, like she's warming up to me. Soon we're discussing anchors, webbing, static ropes, and belay devices. But between the words, we're jousting like fencers to determine one another's rank and knowledge level. By my calculation, it's a draw.

Finally, she hauls her load of webbing and rappel rings to the counter. Absent-minded Uncle Ted doesn't appear right away from the backroom.

"Have you been canyoneering long?" she asks.

"Most of my life." It's what Dad and I did together, along with tracking, but she doesn't need to know that. "And you?"

"Most of my life," she echoes with a bemused smile. "Just moved here two months ago from Lillooet."

An hour away. "And you work for Swallow Canyon Expeditions." I nod at the logo on her T-shirt, the sight of which makes my chest tighten.

"Yup. Ever done Swallow Canyon?"

That question again. "The Upper Canyon a thousand times." *Well, a hundred, anyway.* I lift my chin.

"And the Lower Canyon?"

My chin sinks. I saw the second question coming, but my body goes stiff, anyway.

A smile creeps onto her lips at my reaction, unless I'm imagining it.

"Of course not. You?" I say.

"Once."

As if! "And you came back alive."

"I did." Suddenly, Brigit leans across the counter, her eyes glowing. "I'll take you into the Lower Canyon sometime if you like."

My stomach knots up, and I draw back and stare at her. My first impulse is to spin around and leave her with Uncle Ted, who seems to have forgotten we're even here. But I'm shocked at the part of me that is tempted to accept. Not because I'm suicidal or anything. Maybe just because it has been so long since I've been in any part of Swallow Canyon, or for that matter, had anyone invite me to do anything more than fetch groceries and medicine. Or maybe this Brigit person has some kind of power over people. The way she ordered the firefighters around. The way she just made my uncle feel bad for running a canyoneering and climbing store and not being an expert.

The way she seems to sense my need to escape and have an adventure.

No way. I've got to stick close to Mom.

"Saw your brother's tree-climbing stunt yesterday at school," I say to counter her bizarre offer.

She smiles like there has been no abrupt change of topic. "You were there? I suppose most of the school saw it. Dean has a knack for climbing trees. He got in big trouble for it, like he seemed to be asking for — from school and me. He'll grow out of it soon, I hope."

My father's chair squeaks as Uncle Ted rises and cruises up to the counter. "Sorry, I didn't know you two were waiting for me. Wow, Brigit, you've managed to find quite a few things. I take it Tristan here was useful? Excellent. I'll ring them in. It's a pleasure doing business with Swallow Canyon Expeditions."

"Thanks," she says and looks at me. "Can you help me carry all this to my truck?"

"Of course he will," Uncle Ted tells the best customer he has had in weeks, drowning out my "Yes."

As she unlocks the blue Chevy pickup parked outside, she says, "So, no charge if you want to join the trip I'm guiding Sunday. Could use an experienced hand along."

"To the Lower Canyon?" I ask incredulously.

She laughs lightly. "No, the Upper Canyon, of course."

"Sorry, I'd never get permission for that." My face goes warm for having admitted it. Elspeth is with Mom while I'm at school, but I'm the weekend caretaker. No way can I leave my mom alone an entire day. Who would cook, clean, and listen for when she calls out? Besides, I don't quite get Dean's older sister. Why would she offer a complete stranger a free day trip? Maybe because she has heard about my family? (In small towns, gossip travels fast, even if I've been too out of the loop to hear anything about her.) If that's it and she feels sorry for me, I'm out of here. I don't need anyone's help.

She lifts the pile of canyoneering gear from my arms and tosses it into the back of the pickup.

"You wouldn't get permission? You haven't even asked!"

Then, without a "nice to meet you" or "thanks for the help," she climbs in, slams the driver's door shut, fires up the engine, and drives away. Her ancient mountain bike rattles from where it's tied up in the back.

I'm left standing there, coughing up road dust and scratching my head. A part of me would do anything to canyoneer again — to reclaim the sport I love and miss. Even if it does trigger thoughts that can cut me up like a chainsaw: flashbacks of happy trips with Dad that fight with the crippling memory of the day two grim-faced police officers showed up at our door, and blew up the entire planet.

But anyway, I'm not going to find my way back to the canyoneering world anytime soon. Mom needs me, and she's so fragile. Just the word "canyon" would trigger her.

Of course, I'd never try to explain to her that canyoneering was a special connection Dad and I had. Which is why, despite the tragedy, it's a link to my father that I'll never stop craving.

CHAPTER 4

When I shuffle into the barn at daybreak, my tracker instincts jerk to attention. Something's wrong: the way the hens are cackling and dashing about the hen house.

I stride over to the hens and count. All five are alive and well, even if a little unhinged. Digging into the straw, I collect their eggs. One, two, three.

Two hens haven't laid. Something's up, for sure. *Has a racoon or mink been circling around outside, making them nervous?* Well, it didn't get in or they wouldn't all be here. Anyway, it's a mystery that'll have to wait.

I let the hens out and head back to the house. Placing the eggs on the kitchen counter, I grab a bun to stuff in my mouth and head out the door. Within minutes I've got rabbit tracks in my sights.

Following them, I pause to sniff the spring shoots, listen intensely, and scan the horizon. Left, right, down. Not far into the woods, my superior Spidey sense tells me again that something's not right. The crickets, birds, and soft crackles in the underbrush have stilled, but only immediately around the tree under which I've paused. I scan again: left, right, down. Wait! It's up I'm always forgetting. I raise my head, but a second too late. A blur of beige leaps down from a branch and lands lightly in front of me.

I shake my head at the boy in the beige T-shirt. "Yo, Dean. Why are you trying to scare me, you little jerk?"

Dean can't seem to wipe the smile off his face. "Just having some fun."

"Well, guess what? *Not* funny. And don't you know there are lions, tigers, and bears around here just waiting to eat you up?"

"Yeah? Then why are you here?"

"I'm tracking — following tracks. I'd know if there was a wild animal nearby."

"You didn't spot *me*." He says it triumphantly as he produces a stick of black licorice from his pocket and offers me a piece. It's not your average licorice stick; it has a diameter I could stick an entire finger into. Jumbo licorice.

"True," I admit as I accept the offer. "So, how's climbing club going? And what are you doing here? Does anyone know where you are?"

He shrugs. "What's with the weird cave at your place? The one down by the stream?"

"Been snooping, eh?" I try on a stern tone. "It's called the grotto — it's a fake cave. My dad and I made it from stones and concrete when I was about your age. It's not weird; it's amazing."

"Amazing how?"

"I'll show you."

Ten minutes later, we enter the damp, musty space. The size of a family tent, it resembles a concrete dome that someone inside punched his fist into a hundred times.

"Got lots of dents — er, cubbyholes," Dean says, poking his fingers into some of the cavities in the walls.

"And half of them have a stone in them, all different sizes."

"But what's this cave for?"

"A cool place to hang out, make out, hear your voice echo, and avoid homework. And hide things." I pass my hand over the wall. The rocks in the holes are like ornaments you can rearrange endlessly. "Move the rocks around, and the cave looks different every time. And the hiding spaces change."

"Hiding spaces for what?"

"Easter eggs at Easter time. The marshmallow bunny was always behind the largest rock. Candies at Halloween. The chocolate witch was always behind the largest rock. Little presents at Christmas time. The best one was —"

"— always behind the biggest rock."

"You got it," I say.

He moves about the cave, eyes alight, till he spots the largest stone. It rumbles as he rolls it aside. He turns to me accusingly. "Nothing there."

"Nothing," I agree gloomily. Dad's not around to do it anymore.

Dean rubs his stomach. "Got any food?"

"At home. But you'd have to do some chores for me if you want any." I like how fast I think that up.

"Can you give me a ride to school, too?"

I cross my arms and pretend to consider that a while before I wink. "Lucky for you, my uncle is coming around to pick up my mom this morning. I guess we can stuff you in." Better than having his moody sister show up at our house, if she has any idea where he is. "Come on."

• • •

Dean has fed the chickens, stacked firewood, and polished off three toaster waffles smothered in maple syrup by the time Mom's soft footfalls sound on the stairs. I always feel good seeing her dressed and downstairs, even if it's only for doctor appointments.

"Well, who do we have here?" she asks, all friendly, lifting that numb face of hers and speaking so slowly it almost sounds slurred.

"Dean," I say. "An escaped convict from a nearby prison." I pause for effect. "Kidding. Friend from school."

"Hello, Dean. Did you stay here overnight?"

My attempt at humour has floated right over her, as usual. And she doesn't even seem worried I might have asked someone to stay overnight without her permission. That's way different than the way she was before Dad's disappearance triggered her depression.

He hangs his head slightly. "Yes, in the barn." He doesn't sound apologetic at all — more sly, like he's testing her reaction.

"What?" I say. "So that's what scared the hens. You cost us two eggs. That's fifty-eight cents."

He seems to be studying my mother more than paying attention to me.

"You two thought it would be more fun sleeping in the barn than inside?" Mom asks.

"He —" I start. I can't believe she's so out of it that she thinks I slept in the barn last night.

"Yeah, love sleeping in barn lofts," Dean says.

"Your parents gave you permission to stay over on a school night?" She reaches for a mug and the jar of instant coffee.

He hesitates, then says, "Never had a dad. Mom died last year. Just have a sister."

"Oh." She looks at him with a sympathy that causes him to furrow his eyebrows.

Interesting. I never knew that about Dean, and don't recall anyone in the climbing club mentioning it to me. But I totally understand why he'd hide that information at school.

Mom pours freshly boiled water into her cup and stirs, so slowly that I want to jump up and do it for her.

"You driving us to school?" Dean asks.

"Not me," she replies. "My brother is driving me to the doctor's. But he'll drop you two at school on the way."

"How come you don't drive?" he asks her.

I kick his leg under the table, but he ignores me.

"Our car is broken down, and I don't go anywhere often enough for it to be worth fixing," she says.

It's true.

As she heads down the hall to find her purse, he leans over the last piece of waffle on his fork. "How come she's going to the doctor? Is she sick?"

"How about you shut up and stop asking questions?" I say it nicely.

"Okay, if you answer that one."

"She's — sad."

He nods, like he has already figured it out. "*Very* sad. Better than mad."

I stare at him. *What a strange kid.*

• • •

When Uncle Ted pulls up, I introduce Dean and motion him into the back seat beside me. My uncle steadies my mom's arm as she seats herself up front.

The car has barely made it down the driveway when Dean leans toward me and whispers, "Ask her now."

"*Huh?*"

"Ask her now."

"Ask her what?"

"You know. Permission for the canyoneering trip with my sister." It's barely a whisper.

I grind my teeth. *Did his sister put him up to this? Is that why he appeared out of nowhere this morning?* I stew for a few minutes, then think, *whatever.* Mom's going to refuse no matter when or where I ask her. I feel selfish even trying.

"Mom?"

"Yes, honey." She breaks off from chatting with Uncle Ted about the weather.

"You know school's out this Friday, right? For the summer. And Uncle Ted doesn't need me to start at the shop for a week."

"Yes, dear, Elspeth reminded me."

"Well, I've been invited to go on a hike Sunday. With" — I have to say it — "that group that does canyoneering trips." I don't name the company that competed with my dad when he was running trips from his shop.

"Yeah, my sister's the guide," Dean gushes. "She says she'll take him into the Upper Canyon for free."

What's in it for you? I wonder, studying his eager expression.

"Ah, you're Brigit's brother." Uncle Ted turns to Mom. "Brigit's the new guide over there. I was chatting with Alex Carney, the boss. He says she's good. A reliable type, very experienced, and qualified. Even if she is only nineteen. He has known her for years, since before she moved here recently. How about I spend a day with you, Mary, so Tristan can go?"

Uncle Ted's on my side? Maybe he did hear me when I said I missed climbing club. But I shouldn't have asked, and I shouldn't take off for no reason and tie my uncle up for a whole day.

"Uncle Ted, it's fine —"

"Tristan, I'm so glad you asked," Mom says, though her voice comes out as weak and shaky as a stutter. "Elspeth has been going on about how I need to let you get outside more, about how you'd probably love to go canyoneering. I'm sure Ted and I can manage for a day. If you … if you promise you'll be careful and stay safe."

I can hardly breathe, I'm so stunned. And can only imagine how hard it was for her to say that. So what if it's Elspeth's influence and all to do with her crazy idea? Though, I'm sure she hasn't mentioned her plan to Mom. Still, my mom's actually letting me go? Into the canyon? Not the part of the canyon that took Dad, of course, just the easy part, but, hey, she's giving me a break! Maybe just this once would be okay, if Uncle Ted —

"I agree, Tristan," Uncle Ted says. "If you've been invited and there's no cost, go for it. I'm sure you must miss your canyoneering. You were getting so good."

"Your father said you are going to be one of the best." My mother sniffs and lifts her handkerchief to her face.

"Thanks, Mom," I say, squeezing her shoulder.

"Told you," Dean hisses beside me.

"Are you going?" I ask him.

"Maybe, maybe not," he replies, turning away to stare out the car window.

When Uncle Ted stops outside the school, Dean lifts the door handle and shoots out of the car without a thank-you.

"Hmm," Uncle Ted says. "How do you know Dean, Tristan?"

"Climbing club." I peck my mother's cheek. "Thanks for the ride. Have a good doctor's appointment. See you right after school." I turn to my uncle as I get out of the car. "And thanks, Uncle Ted."

I'm heading for the school steps when Brigit appears out of nowhere, fingers locked on Dean's left ear. She blocks my way but addresses her brother.

"Where were you last night?"

"In Tristan's barn," Dean says, squirming. "Ouch. Lemme go."

Little brat's trying to get me in trouble.

"And why is that?" she demands, looking from him to me.

"Just wanted to see where he lived," Dean says.

"So now that you've seen our estate" — I speak up teasingly — "kindly wait for the gold-embossed invitation before you visit next." I turn to his sister. "I didn't see him till he dropped out of a tree in front of me this morning. He followed me from the barn after freaking out our hens so much they didn't lay."

"Only two of them," Dean corrects me.

"I'm sorry," she says, and her face relaxes. "He sneaks out a lot, but not usually all night, and certainly *not* trespassing on other people's property."

"And asking them for breakfast and a ride to school," I can't resist adding, since it doesn't look like he's in deep enough doo-doo.

Dean gives me dagger-eyes like I'm a traitor. Brigit's frown returns.

"Tristan can go!" Dean says suddenly, brightening. "He got permission from his mom."

I expect her to start in on him again, but she turns an unexpectedly warm smile on me. "Is that true? You're joining our trip on Sunday? That's great news."

I shift from one foot to the other. *Why is it such great news?* I don't even know this woman. *She needs slave labour? Or maybe Dean's coming and she wants a babysitter?*

"I'm honoured to have Julian Gordon's son along. You look a lot like him, you know."

"You knew my dad?" I'm astonished. *She moved here only two months ago from Lillooet, right?* Barely enough time to have heard anything about my family. Obviously too late to have met him. Maybe she just saw a photo in the Lillooet newspaper at the time and noticed 'cause she's a canyoneer, too.

"Anyway, don't worry," she says, like I haven't spoken. "I won't be putting you to work or anything. You'll be a special guest. There are three others joining us: a couple and an experienced canyoneer on vacation from somewhere in Europe."

"Dominik. From Poland," I guess.

Her eyebrows rise. "Oh, you know him? Okay, all the better."

"Is Dean coming?" He's a good enough climber, I figure. But —

"Absolutely not. I've hired a babysitter for him."

"Okay." I wink sympathetically at Dean as he wriggles clear of Brigit's hold like a salmon from an eagle's claws.

I get a quick grin back as he disappears into the wave of students entering the school.

Brigit and I discuss what equipment I'll need, and she gives me directions for when and where to meet up with the group.

"So glad you're joining us, Tristan. See you soon." She beams me one of the sunniest smiles I've had from anyone in months.

I turn and walk into school, both confused and giddy. I'm going on an adventure, and a professional canyoneering guide not only knows I'm alive, but also maybe respects me, has heard that I'm a good canyoneer. I feel myself smiling, really smiling, for the first time in ages.

"Phil!" I shout when I spot my friend. "Guess what!"

CHAPTER 5

The Sunday customers turn out to be Dominik plus some smoochie newlyweds, Harry and Angela Siefkin. Definitely nervous novices, I decide, overhearing the questions with which they pepper poor Brigit and her thirty-five-year-old boss, Alex, during the entire bouncing truck ride to our hike-in point:

"How long is this canyon hike?"

"If we get scared, can we turn back?"

"You'll show us how to put on all this gear, right?"

"Why do we have to wear helmets?"

"Just checking, but you said we'd be back before dark?"

"Relax, you'll love it, and you're with my best guide!" Alex says after answering their questions. "And yes, I'll be at the end point with the truck to pick you up well before dark. Here we are!" He pulls the Chevy up to the trailhead, hops out, and stretches. "Lucky we had such a dry winter, so we can start trips early this year."

A little too early, I'm thinking; Dad would never have put his customers in a stream in June, when the air is still chilly, and there's more chance of a downpour and snow-melt bringing flash floods. Still, I'm not that worried. It's only a little early, and it's only the Upper Canyon.

"Alex is more about profits than safety," Dad used to worry out loud to Mom and me. But I figure he was exaggerating because the two were competitors. "Plus, he spends all his days off going into the canyon alone," Dad would say. "For no reason he'll ever tell me. Fool."

Of course, Alex's guiding service has raked in the dough since Dad disappeared.

"You mean June isn't such a good time to try can-yoneering?" Harry asks, frowning as he and Angela sign release forms that protect Swallow Canyon Expeditions if anything bad happens. Dominik and I, having already signed ours, busy ourselves helping Brigit unload gear.

"I'm just saying we don't usually start up until July," Alex says cautiously, "when water levels in the canyon tend to go down. But this winter has been unusually dry, so you'll be absolutely fine. It's special being on the first trip of the year!"

"Can't wait," I say, my body tingling with excitement as I arrange my wetsuit and ropes in my backpack and strap my helmet on top of it. I can't help feeling like a freed prisoner after a tough fall and winter spent mostly indoors. But I'm also proud of how I've kept Mom and me going. Giving some stuff up — big deal. This day will have been worth the wait.

"Seek out the seed of triumph in every adversity," Dad used to say, quoting some guy named Og.

Alex has said little to me the entire drive; maybe he's a little uncomfortable around me because of his and Dad's relationship, or maybe he feels sorry for me about losing Dad. Anyway, he turns to me now and says, "Glad to see you back at it, young Tristan. Your dad would be proud. How's your mom doing?"

Did I imagine it, or did Brigit just swing around to hear my reply? She's staring at me full-on, as if waiting.

"She's fine," I reply automatically. If I charged twenty-five bucks for every time someone asked me that, I'd make good cash.

"Well, it's a good sign she has let you come along," Alex says.

Is it? I wonder. *I hope so. Or is it just a sign of her being confused and under Elspeth's spell?*

"Angela, do you need help with closing up your pack?" I ask to dead-end that conversation. Coils of un-wound rope are sprouting from the top of her bag like out-of-control dreadlocks.

"Thanks!" she says after I've tucked them in.

"Well, I'm off," Alex informs us. "See you all in a few hours. Have fun!" And he roars off in the truck.

As I move out of the dust he churns up, Brigit calls from a few yards away, "Over here, everyone! Gather around. Safety talk time!"

I lope over and instruct myself to look sharp and in-terested, even if I could pretty much rattle off the safety pointers better than anyone here.

"First, I'm giving you each a whistle," she says.

"Got my own," I let her know.

"Me, too," Dominik says.

Our guide bristles and ignores us. "Tie it to your helmet. It allows us to communicate. If you hear three strong blasts in a row" — she puts lips to whistle and all but shreds our eardrums — "that means there's an emergency. So stop and wait for instructions. One long blast" — my hands clamp over my ears just in time — "that's the all-clear signal. Got it?"

"Got it," Harry says.

She dips her hands into a bag. "I have several sheathed knives here, one for each of you. I'll help you attach them to your —"

"Have my own," Dominik speaks up.

"Me, too," I say as politely as I can.

"— belts, so in the unlikely event of an emergency, you can cut tangled ropes."

Her own knife, I notice, is large and expensive-looking. As she talks on to an attentive Harry and Angela about safe versus unsafe anchors, rappelling technique, and our need to inform her of allergies or medical conditions, my memory surfs back to my father's quiet, patient instruction during each trip, and his infectious joy every time we tackled the Upper Canyon.

What happened, Dad? Where are you? Do you have any idea how much we miss you, and what it has done to Mom?

I remind myself that I've sworn off sad.

"Canyoneering," Brigit continues, "is a way of descending river canyons. Kind of a cross between caving, climbing, and hiking, with some swimming thrown in."

"You mean," Angela pipes up, "we're going to get wet?"

Dominik stifles a laugh; Brigit, to her credit, turns a patient smile on Angela. "Yup, very wet. It's part of the fun. You'll see."

"Oh," Angela says, turning an interesting shade of scarlet.

What was she thinking when she signed up and got fitted for a wetsuit? I wonder, amused.

"You all look quite fit," Brigit says smoothly, "and I know you'll be hooked by the end. Canyoneering is not a well-known sport outside of Europe, but it is getting way more popular all the time. And this area is full of amazing, unexplored canyons."

"What I like about it," I add, "is the way the canyons twist and turn, always downward, like a giant snake. And it's way fun climbing down waterfall faces, if there's not too much water."

"Like playing in a natural water park," Brigit reassures her customers.

"Sounds nice," Harry says, patting his wife's arm.

And then we're off, Brigit leading the way in some brand-new pink canyoneering boots I recognize from our shop, Harry and Angela ambling along the path holding hands, Dominik eyeing the ground for animal tracks. And me? I've turned my face upward to watch eagles soar the thermals, free and graceful against a brilliant blue sky. Song lyrics with the word "freedom" in them start playing in my head.

It's a half-hour's approach to the canyon itself, through forest and meadows rich with foraging deer, leaping squirrels, chattering chipmunks, and chirping birds. Since cameras and cell phones have a way of smashing on canyoneering trips, no one has one outside of their pack, so no one is taking photos.

I find the animal signs all around us as distracting as blinking neon lights, but I keep planting one boot in front of the other. Dominik, on the other hand, soon wanders off course in pursuit of something. He returns with a garter snake dangling from his fingers.

"*Ayiii!*" Angela cries out, backing up.

"This area is full of life," Dominik notes casually, "each with its own special trail." He releases the snake into a nearby bush as Harry gives him the evil eye.

"And some species," Brigit weighs in, "lack thoughtfulness for others." She scowls at the tall European who's a couple of years older than her. He winks back.

As we carry on up an incline, Harry and Angela slow, Harry's breath coming in puffs. Angela pauses frequently to unlace a boot, shake out a pebble, and rub a heel.

"I've got some moleskin I could lend her," I finally suggest to Brigit. The stuff really helps prevent blisters.

"Nope. Some lessons she needs to learn for herself," Brigit says.

Seriously? Brigit's going to purposely let a customer get a blister? It'll only slow Angela down even more. But it seems unwise to defy our guide first thing.

"Hey, Tristan," Dominik calls, motioning me off the path about twenty minutes into our hike.

He points to a little pile of feathers. "A fisher, yes?"

"A fisher," I agree, examining the tracks of the weasel-like creature. "It had a yellow-throated warbler for brunch."

Tracking is like a treasure hunt, following clue to clue. Having a fellow tracker along on the trip today is a definite bonus.

"Look over there," he whispers, pointing. "What is unusual about that vegetation?"

Peering at the bush he's indicating, one surrounded by tall grass, I see nothing at first, not until a breeze stirs. Then I note how the wind strokes only the tops of the vegetation.

"Something's sitting under the bush," I whisper back, pleased with myself.

He nods.

We're sneaking toward it, quiet as outlaws, when I get a strong whiff of body odour. I move my head down to sniff my armpits. Nothing gross there.

"Did you shower this morning?" I whisper to Dominik.

"Yeah, you chump."

"Then the creature we're about to meet is a porcupine."

Dominik halts. "You think?"

"I think faster than you. Porcupines smell like B.O."

"Uh-huh," he agrees.

We back away as slowly as we've moved toward it, just as Brigit calls, "Hey, you two. Are you on this hike or not?"

"We are, boss lady." Dominik flashes a disarming grin her way.

"Good, 'cause we're almost at Swallow Canyon!"

Minutes later the five of us peer down a steep embankment at the creek. We're maybe fifteen feet above the stone's-throw-wide stream, which is running medium-high. It looks just deep enough here to jump down into. Downstream, the twisting canyon walls press the waterway into a series of sparkling pools and frothing drops that disappear around a blind corner.

"We're — we're not going to slide down there on a rope, are we?" Angela asks.

"Nope. We're going to put on our wetsuits and jump in."

"It's the best part of the trip," I encourage her.

"Looks cold," Harry says dubiously.

"That's what the wetsuits are for!" Dominik informs him with enthusiasm. He's already stripping down to his swim trunks and squeezing into his neoprene. As I do the same, Angela and Harry help each other.

"Do I look fat in my wetsuit?" Angela asks her husband with a giggle.

"Cute as an otter," he replies.

"So, we're going to throw our packs down where we intend to jump," Brigit instructs, "then leap in before they float away. One at a time; me first."

I decide to go next, to shut down memories that are rushing into my mind of Dad and me jumping at this very spot, so many times. Holding hands when I was young. Competing for making the largest splash when I was older.

"But how do we know there aren't rocks right under the surface?" Harry asks.

"Great question, Harry," Brigit replies. "We know this spot is generally safe, but there's a chance that stuff can wash in between trips." She's pulling divers' goggles from her pack and nodding at Dominik. "Dominik will serve as my 'meat anchor,' which means he's going to support my weight on the rope. I'll lower myself and when I get to the end of the rope, I slip into the water with my goggles on, check underwater to see whether the pool is safe to jump into, then give you all a signal."

Dominik feeds Brigit's rope around his back and through his hands, then wedges himself firmly against the rocks. "See? This way her body weight cannot pull me down. I look to make sure the rope ends about a foot above the water."

"Why?" Angela asks.

"So the current can't toss the bottom of the rope around or pull Brigit under before she gets free of it," I explain.

"Exactly," Brigit says.

"Oh," Angela says with a brave smile.

Everyone's heads bend as Brigit lowers herself down like a spider on a strand of web, twists like an acrobat to dip her face in the water, then smiles up at us and sticks her whistle in her mouth.

The long single blast entices us to line up at the edge of the cliff like swimmers waiting their turn at a high diving board as Brigit drops from the rope and makes way for us while treading water.

"This is for you, Dad," I whisper as I leap feet-first in my special canyoneering boots — high-traction, shock-absorbing footwear with an inner neoprene bootie — revelling in the rush of air before I bomb into the mind-numbing cold of the creek. When my underwater plunge slows, I open my eyes and lift my arms toward the surface. One little kick, and I rise with patient lungs through a green underworld of bubbles and misty silt clouds.

"*Whoo-hoo!*" Breaking the surface, I emit a cry of pure joy that floats all the way down the deep-throated canyon.

CHAPTER 6

"B-b-balmy!" I shout as the water seeps between my wetsuit and bare skin in an effort to warm itself, flash-freezing my privates before it does so. I lunge for my floating pack and tread water near Brigit, who's smiling approvingly at me, before I grin reassuringly up at the remaining three.

Down comes Angela's flying form. "Uh! Uh! Uh!" she gasps, gulping air as she surfaces, eyes wild and arms thrashing. "C-c-cold!"

"Here I come," Harry announces, leaping where we clear a space for him. He surfaces. "Balmy for Siberia, maybe," he says between convulsive shivers before swimming over to Angela.

"My turn!" Dominik calls down exuberantly. He tucks his rope back in his pack, buckles it shut, tosses the bag down, then performs a show-off back flip.

"Nice one!" I congratulate him as he joins our bobbing party.

"Okay, we're going to float down to the next pool

before there's a place we can get out and walk along the creek again," Brigit informs us.

She gestures to where the water empties down a short, smooth stone chute at the lower end of our pool. Brigit lies on her back, points her feet, and floats toward it, shouting *"Wheee!"*

"C-c-cold," Angela repeats through chattering teeth that fail to hide a smile.

One by one we slide down the chute like kids at a water park — called tobogganing in this sport — then we stand and wade one after the other to the stream's bank. There, we shake water off like a pack of dogs and find a ribbon of dirt beside the shore that's wide enough to walk along.

I spot tracks even before Dominik speaks up.

"A raccoon has been here," he says, squatting down and pointing to imprints that look like a child's hand with pointy nails.

"Did he do the jump and the toboggan?" Harry jokes.

"No. You can see where he waddled down the bank and —"

"Come on, folks," Brigit urges. "We don't have all day to examine every set of animal tracks."

"But over here is wolf scat," Dominik says a minute later, stopping everyone dead.

I should've spotted it before Dominik.

"You're just joking, right?" Angela asks, a tremor in her voice.

I lean down to examine the dog-like stools full of hair. "No worries. Wolves aren't going to come anywhere near us."

"What else should we watch out for?" Harry asks, peering down the pool-drop-pool-drop twists of the canyon.

"There are deer, bears, and cougars up in the forest," Brigit informs them, "but down here, there are fewer and fewer animals the deeper we get into the canyon system. Except maybe bloated carcasses of things that fall in and get washed down."

I feel like she has just knifed me in the gut. I want to scream. *How could she say that within my hearing, knowing —*

The invisible knife twists as she stares back evenly, either trying to interpret my look or defiant. *But why? Is she just stirring the shit?*

"Death, my fellow hikers, is part of nature, part of the circle of life," Dominik says, waving his neoprene-gloved hand about the canyon like a symphony director.

I don't know what Brigit is playing at, but I'm pretty sure Dominik doesn't know that my dad disappeared lower in this canyon. Nor anyone else on this trip. I count to five and breathe deeply to ease the tension in my chest. It works. Soon we're padding in a column along a packed-dirt incline to the sound of tinkling water, scolding blue jays, and the hum of wind through the trees. Within the hour, our path ends abruptly almost two stories above the stream.

"This is the first ledge requiring rope work, everyone," Brigit announces. "So pull out your harnesses, and I'll help you put them on."

I recognize the short, super-easy wall we're about to descend as the place my dad gave me my very first rappelling lessons. Even now I can recall the thrill of donning my first harness, which connects a person's waist and thighs to a rope system. Then, bursting with pride, I lowered myself down this vertical rock face, thinking I was Superman.

"That's my boy! I'm proud of you," Dad said. *Words I'll never hear again.* My throat closes up. I command it to unchoke, which it does.

Everyone searches their backpacks for their harness, a friction device, and carabiners, and Brigit launches into a new talk and demonstration.

"We have two ropes on this hike. One is twice the length of the longest rappel we'll be doing, and the other is our emergency backup. I'll be carrying one. Dominik, I'm assigning you to carry the other."

"Whatever you say, boss," he says cheerfully.

She treats him as her assistant, rather than me, but whatever.

"That way," she explains, "neither he nor I have to carry too heavy a pack. Also, if one pack escapes down the creek, we still have a rappel rope."

"Good thinking," I say.

"Each of us is also carrying shorter rescue ropes enclosed in throw bags, also good in an emergency," she adds.

"What if other canyoneers have left a rope all set up?" Harry asks.

"Excellent question. Be very careful about trusting old anchors, because floods that have washed down since they were set up can make them unreliable."

I shiver. Deep in the Lower Canyon, my father's last anchors sit rusting and shredding through sleet, rain, and floods.

"I'm sorry. I just can't figure this out." Angela's words jerk me back to alertness. She has gotten the leg loops rotated the wrong way on her harness.

"I've got it," says her husband, and he gets her even more tangled.

Dominik raises an eyebrow at me. I try to keep a straight face.

"No worries. I'll help," says Brigit as she strolls over and coaches Angela in a patient, friendly tone.

She's not a bad guide, I decide. Just a slightly strange person, whose reason for inviting me remains a mystery.

Dominik and I are fully rigged by the time Brigit has Angela sorted out. When I start to help Harry, his face turns so crimson that I allow Dominik to step in. *Ha! The guy can't handle a teenager making him look stupid.*

"You've done this before?" Angela asks me.

"Started when I was seven," I say. The words are out before I can stop them. "My dad and I used to do this part of the canyon all the time."

"And he couldn't come today?" asks Harry.

I see Dominik studying me, and Brigit turns my way again. I can't read her expression. Suddenly, I'm pissed off that Brigit does nothing to stop these questions. She must know the story, given she works for Alex and told me I look like my dad.

"Nope" is all I say. It comes out a bit croaky.

No point being pissed off. Just deal with it. It will get easier. It has to.

"I'll lower myself first," Brigit informs us. "Then I'll signal up. Dominik, you go last, please."

I figured she'd say that. First and last down are always at slightly higher risk than the rest, so the most experienced — she and Dominik, in her opinion — take those positions. The first down doesn't know what to expect, so has to rely on others lowering them down. The last one, on the other hand, has no one to back up their anchor, so they need the experience to make sure the rope doesn't get twisted or caught. Only when everyone's down does the leader pull the rope free.

"This, everyone, is a circle of webbing," Brigit says as she places a piece around a small but secure boulder. "It's going to serve as my anchor. And see this thing that looks like a necklace pendant on the downward side? That's called a 'quicklink.' Watch as I feed my rappel rope through it."

"Interesting," Harry says dutifully.

"Mmm," says Angela as the rest of us nod.

"Now, on one side of the rope I'm attaching a carabiner. See how the rope slides through the quicklink? That allows it to pull only one way. It works like a belt buckle: the quicklink 'blocks' if the rope is yanked the opposite way."

"Clever," Harry says.

Next she feeds the other end of the rope through a fancy figure-eight-type configuration just above where it's attached to her harness. "And this set-up lets me control how fast I descend. It offers the resistance I need."

"Hmm," says Angela.

"Okay. Here's the fun part, folks." Brigit proceeds to "walk" down the cliff face with feet to the wall, face to the sky, holding one strand of the rope in her gloved hands.

I speak up. "Notice how there's no knot on the end of the rappel rope. That's different than in climbing."

"Why?" Harry asks.

"Because when you get to the end, sometimes you have to get clear of thrashing water real fast, so that you don't drown," I explain.

"Drown?" Angela repeats nervously.

"It gives you more control, but it also means you have to pay attention. Because you want the rope's end to stay above the water, but you also have to know exactly when you're going to run out of rope and fall into the drink." An old expression of my Dad's I kind of like.

"Bravo, Tristano," Dominik says. "Guide Brigit had better watch her cute little behind."

That's rude, man, I think. Anyway, no way Brigit has to worry about Alex hiring me over her.

A long, clear whistle sounds from below.

"All clear," Angela says. "It means we go next, right?"

"Exactly. Dominik and I will help you," I assure her.

"Yahoo!" I cheer minutes later as I splash into the creek — shallower here than the last place we jumped in — after Harry and Angela. We swim aside and wait for our Polish friend to land.

"*Tak!*" he shouts in glee when he surfaces. "That's 'yes!' in Polish."

"So now," Brigit says, taking over again, "I pull the rope from the unblocked pull side, so that it falls free."

"But —" Harry points up to the bank we just leaped from.

"Yup, this system leaves the webbing around the boulder. No big deal. Another canyoneering party might use it, if no floods shred it before they find it. And once I pull the rope," she reminds us, giving it a dramatic tug, "there's no going back. Canyoneering is all about going down, not up."

"No going back," Angela repeats soberly, shaking and looking at Harry.

"Wow," he says, "coming down on that rope was pretty intense."

Chill, you guys, I want to say. *Just enjoy yourselves!* Rappelling is one of the easiest, most fun parts of the sport — at least, when someone else sets you up. Harry and Angela should be pumped about the experience. Dominik and I trade looks. *Could be a slow day.*

We step out of the water, then follow Brigit down a path beside the stream, pausing to enjoy the view of the sparkling water, its mossy log-jams and dancing currents.

"So, Tristan," Brigit says as she moves up to walk beside me, "how long since you've been down here?"

I hesitate. "Eight months."

"Makes sense. You were looking a little rusty earlier this morning, but you've already got your rhythm back."

Not sure it's true, but sounds good to me. I force a smile.

"*Ouch!*" Her angry cry startles me as she examines her arm. "A wasp just stung me."

"You okay?" Dominik and I ask at the same time.

"Yes, but it's time to stop for a cup of tea," she says unexpectedly, glancing at a nearby tree stump over which a dozen wasps hover.

"Now?" I ask, surprised anyone would want tea in the midday warmth, especially near a wasps' nest.

"Yes!" she snaps, and in no time she has extracted her camping stove to heat up a pot of creek water. Strangely, she also dons a hooded sweatshirt and pulls the hood tight around her face.

As the pot bubbles fiercely, I organize tea bags and cups. Suddenly, she rises, grips the pot handle, sprints over to the stump, and pours the steaming water on the wasps' nest.

Angela's blood-curdling scream — *a fear of the wasps coming after her?* — prompts Harry to wrap his arms around her and haul her well away from the stump. Dominik and I are preparing to dive into the stream when I realize that few of the wasps survived the attack, and none are coming for us.

Brigit marches toward us, a triumphant look on her still-hooded face. "That'll teach them," she says.

"But only one stung you," Dominik objects.

"The rest had to pay for that," she declares flatly. "Now, anyone *really* want tea or shall we carry on?"

CHAPTER 7

"Remind me not to get on that girl's bad side," Dominik jokes quietly as we amble behind the rest of the group a short while later.

"She's a little unpredictable," I agree cautiously. *More like frenetic as a mad hen.* "But nice of her to invite me."

"She is impressed with you. When I was walking with her just now, all she could talk about was what a great canyoneer you are."

"Me?" My face goes warm. "I hardly know her. This is our first trip together."

"Well, she seems to know all about you. And she told me about your mom and dad. So sorry —"

I stiffen. "She has no right to tell anyone stuff about me."

"Easy, kid. I just said it so you do not feel you have to hide anything."

"What exactly did she say?" I demand.

Dominik shuffles his feet and steals a glance at our companions. Brigit is absorbed in pointing out plants and offering some kind of nature lecture. She and the couple are definitely out of earshot.

"She said your dad drowned in the canyon last fall, and your mom has not been okay since. And that you never get out canyoneering anymore."

I feel the colour drain from my face. "My mother's getting better," I lie. "I look after her because I've got to. So what?"

"Very noble of you, Tristan," Dominik replies. "Please do not be cross about Brigit telling me. She may be moody, but she is a nice girl at heart. We've been talking, and I've learned she has been through family troubles herself, so maybe she understands."

"Understands what?"

He rubs his chin. "Look, I have obviously said too much already. She helped you get out canyoneering to-day, right? And she is impressed by your abilities. Let us just leave it at that."

I lower my pulse by watching the water flow beside us. Then I raise my head to appreciate a burst of ferns sprouting from a crack in the canyon wall. My eyes continue up twelve stories to the top of the canyon wall.

Tensing, I grab Dominik's elbow. "Look up there, on the rim. Do you see something?"

He raises his head and squints. "Nope. Why?"

"I saw a person and a flash of light, like a signal."

"Signal? Sorry, Tristan. I do not see anyone up there."

I look again at where I'm sure I saw the silhouette of a figure and the glint of sun off glass. Nothing there now. Whoever was there has done a disappearing act.

"Someone is up there watching us with a pair of binoculars," I speculate. "Or else they used a mirror to signal us."

Dominik is peering at me. "Could be a house, a car, maybe even a hiker checking out the canyon. Or maybe the glint in the eye of that cougar, who likes you so much that he is tracking you again." He's smiling.

"Nice try, but no houses, roads, or trails up there."

"Dominik! Tristan! I've seen snails move faster than you two," Brigit shouts. "Can't keep up with the rest of us?"

He and I exchange looks again and speed up.

"We're almost to Emerald Pool," she enthuses as we approach. "We can have our picnic lunch there. Then there are three short, easy waterfall descents before our exit out of the Upper Canyon. If we miss that exit, we enter the Lower Canyon."

"The Lower Canyon is more difficult?" Harry asks.

"Ten times more difficult. Not many people are capable of doing it. We'll not be going there today," she says in her friendly guide voice, which I'm starting to believe is not her real voice.

"The Lower Canyon," Angela repeats slowly, pressing a finger against her chin. "Isn't that where some woman drowned last fall? And a guy went missing? Sounds really dangerous."

My body goes as tense as steel. I notice Brigit's eyes narrow before she dons her guide face again. She doesn't look my way. She's clearly avoiding looking my way.

"The woman's body washed up," Harry contributes helpfully. "The guy's was never found. But I can't remember if they were connected."

"I think we should stick to cheerful topics," Brigit says in a pleasant but measured tone. "And we should proceed to the pool, which will be the best part of today."

Emerald Pool lives up to its name, tranquil and green. Plumes of vapour hover over the top lip of the short chute that feeds it. One by one, we toboggan down the spillway with whoops of delight and then float on our backs for a minute in the peaceful stretch of water, gazing at the sky. To one side, a branch loaded with leaves sticks out of a crack in the canyon wall, like an exotic sun umbrella. Above it, a series of thick branches from a large hemlock tree elbow out of the rock face.

"So," Dominik says as he lodges himself two tree branches above the water and starts eating the sandwich Brigit has passed him. "How long have you been canyoneering, Brigit?"

"Since I was a kid." Seated on a riverside boulder across from one I've claimed beneath the tree, dangling a foot in the green water, she takes a large bite from her apple.

"Your dad got you started?" Harry asks from his perch below Dominik as he rips into his potato chip bag.

"Never had a dad. Learned from my mom," Brigit answers after some hesitation.

"Your mother was a canyoneer?" Angela exclaims. Poised standing at one end of the tree's bottom limb, sandwich in hand, she shuffles along it like she's a gymnast on a balance beam, lifting one foot at a time as she moves toward Harry. Though she's only a few feet above the water, I don't relax until she plunks herself down on the lowest branch beneath her husband's swinging legs. That's when I notice murky water flow into the clean green water from the chute. It unsettles me enough that I almost don't catch Angela's next question: "So how'd your mom get into it?"

"She was a geologist. Her work took her into canyons." Brigit's voice has an edge to it, as if she's resentful of the questions.

"Does she still do canyoneering?" I ask, remembering only after the question is out of my mouth that Dean said their mom died last year.

She turns hard eyes on me and her "No!" comes out ice-cold, flashing me back to that day at school when she stared menacingly at me.

"Do you take Dean canyoneering?" I press, willing to piss her off as payback for her talking to Dominik behind my back.

To my surprise, instead of inflaming her, this transforms her expression into one of softness and pride. "Dean is amazing. Smart as anything and an awesome climber. And yes, he has been in the Upper Canyon several times with me. Never in the Lower, of course. Sometimes he misbehaves, but that's a twelve-year-old boy for you." She smiles glowingly, the proudest sister I've ever met.

"You don't look old enough to have a twelve-year-old," Angela declares, raising her voice to compete with the sudden splashing of a log and some debris down the waterslide.

"He's my brother," Brigit corrects her client in a gentle tone. "I'm his guardian. We have each other for family. Do *you* have kids?" she addresses Angela and Harry, clearly ducking further questions about her life.

Angela reaches up to clasp Harry's hand and smiles. "We only got married last month. So someday, maybe. In —"

"— a flash!" I say.

"Pardon?" Harry stares at me.

"A flash, up there." My finger points to the forest floor high above us.

"Tristan keeps seeing flashes from the rim," Dominik explains, "like sun hitting binoculars. He thinks someone is stalking us." The teasing voice prompts me to lower my head for a second.

"*Shh!*" I order, suddenly noticing the spread of mucky water, floating branches, and bark pieces spoiling our pretty pool.

"Like you can hear someone from way up there —" Dominik starts. Then he goes quiet and also stares at the new jumble of debris floating around our pool. Brigit, Dominik, and I all leap up at the same time.

"Get up the tree, high as you can go!" Brigit shouts before blowing three loud shrieks on her whistle.

As I scramble up to the first branch, I tie a rope to my harness and form an alpine butterfly knot to clip into Angela's harness. Only as the carabiner clicks into place do I realize that Brigit has done the same from the other side. Then we're on the second, the third, the fourth branches of the tree growing out of the rock wall.

Dominik leapfrogs all the way to a high, sturdy branch in seconds.

Brigit pauses just under him. "Move it, Angela!" she shouts, as she and I position ourselves beside one another for rope hauling. Harry offers his arm down to his shrieking wife as he scrambles upward, but they're not moving fast enough.

From faraway upstream comes an ominous rumble.

Wordlessly, Brigit and I begin to pull Angela up on the ropes secured to her. We strain and yank and tug as the thunderous growl speeds toward us. Then a wave of muddy water bursts down the chute and infiltrates Emerald Pool. We stare, mesmerized, as the fast-moving head of muddy water fronted by debris snakes toward us like a dark, multi-armed monster.

Faster and faster it moves, its head gobbling up any debris in its way, its arms shifting left and right according to the pond's shape. With every foot that it progresses, it grows faster and more powerful. Behind it rides an astonishing volume of lighter brown water that takes over all in its path, hoisting up logs, covering boulders, rising as it gulps its way downstream.

Emerald Pool transforms into a raging, mud-coloured whirlpool. The roiling water soon reaches Angela's dangling shoes. Dominik pulls Harry up beside him; Brigit and I exert full force on the ropes securing his wife.

"Help me! Help me!" Angela cries even after she's wrapped safely in Harry's arms.

All of us are clinging to our trembling tree branch.

In minutes, the force is spent, and the roar dies down as the head of foaming brown water continues downstream.

"*Whaa — ?*" Harry says.

"Flash flood," I explain, while Brigit — who I have to admit handled the crisis admirably — makes sure everyone has a secure grip. "Is everyone okay?"

It wasn't Brigit's or Alex's fault, I remind myself. Alex may have started the season slightly early, but no one can predict a freak flash flood; they can only ensure that the guide is experienced and capable enough to react swiftly and correctly if it does happen. Which she did.

"Yes, but where did that water come from? It's blue sky, no rain," Angela says, both hands gripping her husband's arm.

"Doesn't need to rain here to raise the stream level," I explain. "If it rains far upstream, it doesn't take long to reach us."

"And you heard it coming?" Harry's face is white.

"No. First the water goes brown, then stuff starts coming down. By the time you hear a flash flood coming, it's too late," I reply. I can hardly believe I recognized the signs before Brigit and Dominik.

"Thanks for helping me with your ropes," Angela mumbles. "You maybe saved my life."

"You're welcome," Brigit and I say at the same time.

"What a story we'll have to tell when we get back, right, Harry?" Angela sounds almost excited now that the drama is over.

"Mmm," Harry says, observing the torrent beneath us. "How do we get out of here now?"

Dominik, Brigit, and I eye the crack from which our tree thrusts. The maze of branches almost resembles a beanstalk, ending at a point about two-thirds of the way up the canyon wall. After that, the crack is more like a chimney, which I calculate even Angela can scramble up with a little coaching.

"We should —" Brigit starts.

"— make like Jack and the Freakin' Beanstalk," I finish for her, ignoring the annoyed look it puts on her face.

"We are lucky," Dominik rules.

"Yes. We have branches, ropes, ascending gear, and an easy crack to climb up," Brigit agrees. "I also have a cell phone in my pack for contacting Alex to meet us up at the trailhead."

So, this day trip is going to end abruptly, I reflect, as we begin scrambling upward. Safely for the five of us, thankfully. But with no clues as to why I was invited.

CHAPTER 8

"How was it?" Mom asks the next day, holding my hand as she settles back against her pillows.

"Amazing! There was a nice guy who's a tracker and a honeymooning couple you'd have liked. The weather was perfect, the trees are all sprouting buds and — well, it has been a long time since I was out, so I really appreciate your letting me go." I judge it less than wise to mention the excitement of the flash flood. "What did you and Uncle Ted get up to?"

"Oh, Ted needed to do things at the shop," she says. "So he arranged for Elspeth to drop in with her boy. And the boy read to me while Elspeth ran errands. It was lovely."

"But, Mom — Elspeth doesn't have a kid." Guilt hits me sledgehammer-like for being away having fun while some strange kid read to my bedridden mom. I look around her room and spot one of my joke books half open on her nightstand, bookmarked with a stick of jumbo black licorice.

"You're right, Tristan. It was just a boy she was babysitting. A nice boy. Seemed like I had met him before."

I rise and pick up the licorice between my thumb and forefinger like a police officer collecting evidence at a crime scene. "So, Uncle Ted jams on looking after you, and Elspeth, who is being paid to look after someone else, shows up and dumps her babysitting job on you. What was this boy's name, Mom?" *Negatory detect-o-meter activating.*

Mom sighs and closes her eyes. "Sorry, Tristan, I don't remember."

"Dean?"

"Mmm, that sounds right. He was a nice boy. Okay if I sleep now, honey?"

Squeezing her hand, I exit the room. In the kitchen, I open and close cupboards. They're as empty as when I left. *Got to get us some food.* The money tin turns out to be empty: Uncle Ted still hasn't gotten around to refilling it. After tiptoeing upstairs, I open Mom's purse as she snoozes. I take the only card that still works, and hop on my bike for town.

• • •

At the grocery store, I grab two cans of baked beans, the cheapest loaf of bread, and a carton of milk, then punch in the code my mother trusted me with the week after Dad disappeared.

"Sorry, card declined," a freckled cashier woman informs me.

"But that's impossible. There should be —" My face burns hot. I push the food back at her and flee, my stomach rumbling big time. At high speed, I pedal all the way to my dad's — er, uncle's — store.

"Closed," the sign declares.

"What?" I say out loud, cupping my hands around my eyes to peer into the darkened interior. My sweaty fingers slide down the glass.

• • •

It's only a few blocks to the garage where Uncle Ted used to work. I cycle over and immediately recognize his scuffed safety boots sticking out from under a car.

"Uncle Ted?"

A hand holding a wrench appears from under one side of the car. Then the boots wriggle toward me. "Tristan! You're back. How was the canyon?"

"It was great. Thanks for letting me go. And Mom's fine. But Uncle Ted, there's no money in the tin, no money in the bank, and no food in the house! And why are you here and not at the store?"

Uncle Ted sits up, grease smears on his face, and frowns at me.

"Tristan, the account has been low for a long time, and I've been buying most of your food from what I can earn here when I'm not at your dad's shop. The canyoneering store has been losing money for months, son. So I've reduced its hours, and I close up when I get called in for some work here."

I stare at him, unable to move. "What are you saying, Uncle Ted?"

"I'm sorry, very sorry, Tristan. I'm just not cut out to manage a retail store. It's time we close it down and sell what inventory we can. You'll need to get a job to support the two of you."

"But you didn't want to cut back Elspeth's hours when we talked last week."

He hangs his head. "I honestly didn't know how bad things were until I took a tally while you were away yesterday. I'll pay the last of Elspeth's wages and put a little into the account, but the last few months have been tough on me, too, Tristan. I'm struggling to support the three of us, and I can't keep it up. I'm just telling you like it is. If only Mary would —" He stops, lays his wrench on the concrete floor, and drops his chin to his chest.

My feet take an unsteady step back; my chest has seized up. Mom and I are broke? Unless I drop out of school and work like a madman. Or unless Mom pulls herself together and gets her job back at the bakery.

Uncle Ted is still sitting with slumped shoulders on the stained concrete floor. "I've let you down, Tristan. But I'll keep trying. There's always government assistance if you want me to help you with the paperwork. And I'll give you a solid reference for any job you —"

"Hey!" comes a shout from the back of the garage. "Ted, I'm not paying you to socialize, and that car's not going to repair itself."

I breathe in slowly, then exhale. Fear has displaced the hunger in my stomach. That, and a stab of despair.

Uncle Ted's dejected figure is becoming blurred. My running shoes take another step back.

"It's okay, Uncle Ted," I manage to say. "I'll figure something out."

Then I'm on my bike, my feet working the pedals toward home. A vision of rushing upstairs and shaking my mother to her senses comes over me. *Mom, Mom, get up and get a job! Be alive again! Lying here won't bring Dad back. I can't keep doing everything! He would want us to pull together.*

But wouldn't you know there is a certain moped in the driveway. And there's its owner, standing in my mother's apron, hands on her hips in the doorway and a wooden spoon in her hands.

"Tristan! Just in time for my lasagne. I made it at home, and I'm just zapping it in your microwave this minute. I'm betting we can convince your mom to eat some. What do you think?"

Okay, no need to say anything till I've eaten. And it's true that she's better than me at coaxing Mom to eat. I sit down at the table. "Thanks."

As I chow down, she watches me with a satisfied grin.

"Tristan, your uncle has told me I'm laid off, but you know what? I'm so fond of your mother and you that I'm willing to keep coming around sometimes for no pay. Lord knows you both need a good home-cooked meal now and again. But what's really important, as you know, is that you get into the canyon again and bring back that special token. The sooner, the better."

My fork stops halfway to my mouth. An eye-roll is threatening to unleash itself. I'm trying to decide how to respond, when there's a loud knocking at the door.

"For you, probably." Elspeth rises, takes the small plate of lasagne she has served up for Mom and heads up the stairs.

"Dominik?" The last person I expect.

"Hey, Tristan, I asked around until I found out where you live. Was wondering if you would like to come tracking with me tomorrow. Because you are out of school now, right? And it is not like I know anyone else in town, tracker or otherwise."

He's looking around our living room, smelling the lasagne, no doubt taking in all the messes I have on my list to clean up. He's also peering covertly at the stairs as if wanting a glimpse of my sickly mom.

"I can help you with some chores or something if that is what it takes for you to get out." My stunned silence makes him stop peering about. "I mean, it is more fun to track with someone than on your own, yes?"

I picture Dominik and me tracking wildlife along the rim of the canyon. Then I envision me looking down, spying my father's bright orange backpack hanging neatly from a branch sticking out of the canyon wall, and reaching down to retrieve it. Is that really what it would take to get my mom to rise and shine — to support us till I graduate and find someone to help us make the shop turn a profit again? Or am I just starting to think like crazy Elspeth?

Elspeth's red clogs appear on the upper stair landing. "Tristan, I couldn't help overhearing. I'll cover things here tomorrow while you do that, okay? And I'll have a meatloaf and apple pie on the table for you when you get home."

I'm torn, but not for long. *It's for Mom, not me.*

"You're on," I tell Dominik.

CHAPTER 9

"Thanks for helping me clean the barn," I say as we drive off in Dominik's little red rental car the next morning. I can hardly believe all the work he did to get me out of the house: replaced some rotten boards on our deck, hauled some junk from the barn and to the dump, and even fixed the washing machine while I scrubbed the bathroom and kitchen floors.

"No problem. Had to do all that stuff growing up, too. Who is the hippie lady who looks after your mother?"

Be positive. "Someone my uncle came up with. I can't leave my mom for very long, so she helps out. And she makes pretty good food when she feels like it."

"Hmm. Saw her with Alex the other day in town. Brigit's boss."

I shrug. "It's a small town. Most people know each other."

A while later, Dominik parks at the trailhead, and we clamber out. We've hiked for less than ten minutes when Dominik bends down.

"So, what do you say these tracks are?"

I study the small rounded footpads featuring five oval toe marks with pinprick claw marks on the ends. An imprint of stiff hairs fills out the impression. "Something in the weasel family."

"*Tak.*"

"Skunk?"

"Good man. Male or female?"

I lean down closer to compare front and back footprints. Since the hind feet are slightly to the outside of the front feet, and female skunks' wider pelvises make them waddle like my three-hundred-pound Great Aunt Hilda, I say, "Female."

"Okay, I am impressed. How old are the tracks? And what is this skunk's story?"

"Skunks are nocturnal, and the tracks aren't many hours old, so I'm guessing they're from last night. She was tracking a grasshopper," I note, pointing at the faint grasshopper trail: sets of offset diagonal dents in the dust with an in-between line of horizontal dashes.

"Wow, someone taught you well. Your turn to test me."

I spot a tree with a large hollow at its bottom and point to it. "What lives there?"

Dominik wanders over to it, gets down on hands and knees, and pulls out a flashlight and magnifying glass. He sticks his head in and sniffs while directing the light and magnifier on tracks and hairs. "A squirrel, no big surprise."

"Come on, what type of squirrel?"

He does an exaggerated sigh and pulls out a ruler to measure various prints. "Used to be a ground squirrel, but a grey one seems to have booted him out. And the new resident has been nibbling on a small snake, judging from the fragments in his scat."

"What kind of snake?"

"Oh, give me a break, kid." Dominik grins. "How are you at tracking people?"

"Not my specialty," I claim, unwilling to tell a Search and Rescue professional that Dad and I used to play trackers' hide-and-seek for hours in the woods. I especially won't admit the weirdest advice Dad ever gave me for tracking large animals or people: hide in a mud hole, breathing through a reed. And if you're playing with a friend, rise suddenly to surprise him as he passes by.

Dad played that on me once, and I smile at the memory.

"Okay, give me five minutes, then try to find me," he says, winking.

"You're on."

I sit down in the hollow of the tree, close my eyes and spend five minutes trying to identify the multitude of smells in the musty, rotting home. At the agreed-on time, I amble through the woods, following broken twigs, upturned stones, and the occasional portion of a footprint. At first his trail is obvious; he's purposely crashing through bushes and walking like someone who doesn't know how trackers work.

Soon he starts covering his trail like a pro. But I've done enough tracking to keep on him. Like a cat creeping up on a bird, I move slowly without sudden movements, my arms and hands close to my body. Each step is so slow-mo that I make almost no sound. At one point, when I think I've lost him, I place my ear against a flat stump, which is a natural conductor of sound — as good as an echo chamber, my dad used to say. With this method, I identify the slightest footfall a good distance to my left, but at the same time, a distinct crackle in the brush well to my right.

I jerk my head up, confused, and stare to the right. Someone or something is following both of us, and my senses tell me it's a human being. And yet — I grin. Clever Dominik thinks I don't know about the rock-tossing trick that can make a follower veer the wrong way.

Still pausing, looking both left and right, I notice I'm only feet from the canyon rim. The Lower Canyon rim. My feet move there on their own; Dominik's and my game can continue in a minute, after I've peeked over the edge. I lie on my belly and stare down several storeys into the depths. The pungent smell of dirt and vegetation rises to my nostrils; shadows play off the boulders, and I can just hear the trickle of water at the bottom. Tangles of roots form a sort of ladder halfway down the slope beneath my chin. And —

Something red — *red?* — is hanging on one of the last loops.

I slide forward, head and chest now hanging over the gradual drop-off, trying to identify the item. *My father wore a red bandana. Was he wearing it the day he disappeared?*

Could he have tried to climb up this very face? Could this red piece of cloth be what's left of his bandana?

I have no binoculars or canyoneering gear, but on impulse this morning I stuck a thick, non-technical rope into my backpack. I'm suddenly obsessed with a need to get a closer look at the thing. I check around for a natural anchor. The only option is a boulder the size of a beach ball; there's a scattering of smaller rocks beside it. After pushing and pulling on the boulder to make sure it's not going to move, I place my rope around the boulder's neck and start working my way down.

I'm trusting that the boulder as anchor, my superi- or upper body strength, the rope, and the tree roots will allow me to scramble back up the slope, while my lock-hold on the rope will keep me from falling. In real- ity, I know it's a little crazy, sliding down a drop without companions or proper stuff. But what if the tiny scrap of red was my father's? A chill runs down my back.

Lower and lower I go, my running shoes loosing dirt showers, my sweaty palms greasing the rope. I twist my head around every now and then to sight the scrap. Slowly, way too slowly, I draw near. All that's clear is that it's small, faded, half-shredded, and red. Maybe a ban- dana, maybe not. I've got to actually examine it in my hand. *How did it get halfway up a cliff wall, anyway? And how long has it been here?* I'm at the end of my rope, but if I re- lease it for a second and trust my heels to a lower stirrup of roots, and reach, reach down with my left hand —

"What the —" I scream as a shower of dirt rains on me from above. I push my head into a small cavity in the cliff, trying to protect my skull from whatever might come loose next. It's a good thing I do, because the next avalanche is small rocks pouring down, several glancing off my sweaty shoulders, more unsettling than painful.

The loop of roots securing my feet breaks as I wriggle to flatten my body against the cliff face, and for a second, my hands cling to a too-small root while my feet flail for a hold. *What was I thinking, going lower than my rope?* An even lower root finally decides to hold one foot, but now my arms, still clinging to another root, are stretched like bungee cords. From afar, I must look like a large spider cowering under a gushing bathtub spout.

The little avalanche runs out of fuel. My desperate foothold and panicked handhold remain secure, if tiring. Slowly, delicately, I find even lower handholds and footholds, then look down to see that one foot has actually come to rest on the root holding the cloth. *Bingo!* But my movement has freed it, and now it's floating, ever so slowly, toward the bottom of the canyon. From the way it's drifting, I can see now that it's not cloth but paper: a picnic napkin probably caught in a small wind gust as people sat eating on the boulder above.

Idiot. Nearly killing yourself for a napkin. My desire for a clue to my father's disappearance had overruled my common sense. Even if it had been Dad's bandana, I should've waited for Dominik to help me. Or come back tomorrow with binoculars.

Gingerly, I work my way back up to the bottom of the rope, then put all my strength into pulling myself up it. Visions of gym class flash through my mind. Palms tightly around the rope, I continue to climb, hand over moist hand, tentative toeholds in the roots helping.

"Tristan?" A voice sounds from above as I come within arm's reach of the top.

I stare up at the welcome sight of Dominik's face. "I'm just hanging out here, but I could use a hand."

"*Tak*, I guess you could, you demented devil." His bulging biceps hoist me up like a powerful mechanical crane arm.

Taking a deep breath as I lie on solid ground, I stare at the boulder that served as my anchor. The pile of rocks beside it is gone. All gone, now sitting at the bottom of the canyon. But the small rocks were never right beside the edge. *Had someone moved them? But who?* I vaguely recall wondering earlier if someone was following us.

"You okay?" Dominik asks, eyebrows puckered. "And you will award me with an explanation?"

"Yes, but that slide wasn't natural," I say, raising myself to my hands and knees and crawling around the boulder in search of footprints.

"A slide? Stuff fell on you?" Dominik examines my head and shoulders. "You seem okay. But why would you go over the edge at all? You are a moron if you think my trail led down there!" He shakes his head. "And what do you mean it is not natural? That's what cliffs do. They erode and send rocks and dirt down sometimes. It is why we wear helmets when canyoneering. But we did not come here to canyoneer today, as I understand it. So why did you have a rope in your pack, anyway?"

He sits back on his haunches and waits for answers.

"I'm sorry," I say, ashamed for having lowered myself over the cliff, and at a loss to explain why I had brought a rope. "I — I thought I saw something down there, caught on the wall." He stares at me for a long time, until I add, "Something of my dad's."

His face softens.

I stare at the ground. "But it wasn't anything to do with him."

"And you brought the rope just in case."

"S-sort of."

He punches my shoulder gently and unties my rope from the boulder. "Let us head home, Tristan. Your mother needs you. I will buy you a cola on the way."

CHAPTER 10

"Mom, wake up. We have to talk."

"She has been sleeping all day," Dean informs me as he stands staring at the family photos on her dresser, his hands jammed into his jeans pockets. "Like, all she ever does is sleep."

"You've been here all day?" My fault for trusting Elspeth, selfish dipshit that I am. *But since when is it responsible for Elspeth to leave a twelve-year-old in charge?*

"Yeah. For twenty-five bucks." He grins like he just won the lottery.

"And when will Elspeth be back?" *For me to strangle.*

He shrugs. "Who knows?"

"Tristan?" Mom mumbles.

"Yeah, Mom, it's me. I'm back." I sit beside her on the quilt.

"Back from where?" She looks muddled, prompting a stab of guilt in me.

"Tracking, Mom."

"Lucky you," Dean says with his elfish grin.

Mom pats my hand and closes her eyes again.

"Mom, please, can you concentrate for a few minutes?" I say softly.

She makes an effort to prop herself up and asks for a glass of water. Dean has it in her hands before I manage to rise.

"Oh, hello, Dean. Have you met my son, Tristan?"

I frown, but tell myself she's just sleepy. Or dopey from too many drugs.

"What is it you need to talk about, dear?"

"Dean, can you please leave us alone for a few minutes?"

"I'll only listen from the other side of the door."

My flash of annoyance fades to amusement. The kid's honest, got to give him that. *Who cares what he hears, anyway?*

"He's lovely, dear. Let him stay," Mom says, patting my hand again.

I cough to clear my throat, then dive into the speech I've rehearsed all the way home from the tracking trip.

"Mom, I've decided I'm going into the Lower Canyon to try to find some sign of what happened to Dad."

She sits up straighter and digs her fingers into my arm. "No, no, no, Tristan! *Pleeeease.*"

"Mom, I know Search and Rescue found a few things, but this is something I've got to do. So I need you to remind me what he was wearing the day he left and stuff like that." I've racked my own brain but have little memory of his departure. After all, he went canyoneering a lot, and no one, including him, could have expected that goodbye to be his last.

She bursts into sobs and hides her face in the pillow. Dean runs a finger through the layer of dust on her bedside table, then cocks an eyebrow at me.

I look away and find myself gazing at her open closet, where Dad's boots and shoes are lined up neatly, all polished by Mom before that fateful day. I know the sole imprint of each and every piece of footwear he wore while tracking with me. How we loved stalking each other around the woods, from the time I could barely walk. Only one pair is missing: the black canyoneering boots he wore into the Lower Canyon last October.

Pulling my eyes away from Dad's stuff, I wait until Mom's tears have spent themselves, then I repeat my request more gently.

Between occasional sobs, she finally says, "The green sweater I knitted for him, his light yellow windbreaker, his black canyoneering boots. His usual wetsuit and gear, and his red bandana."

"That's good, Mom. And his orange backpack?"

She nods as more tears fall. "I told all that to Search and Rescue, Tristan. Don't try to do their job. It would be dangerous. And I don't want to lose you, too."

I sigh, torn and racked with concern for her. "I know this is hard for you, Mom, but what else can you remember? Is there anything you didn't tell me before? About where he said he was going, who with, and why?"

The sobs turn into violent moans and thrashing. Dean's eyes widen, then he slinks out the bedroom door.

"Mom," I whisper, my face near hers as my hands clutch hers. "Please calm down. Just answer that question, and I won't ask any more."

"He — your father" — she gestures toward her dresser — "left his wedding ring behind."

She slides under her covers, flops over, and buries her head so far into her duck-down pillow that I fear she'll smother herself. Her hands are balled into fists that are making feathers fly out of the pillow.

I walk over to the jewellery case on their dresser and check. Sure enough, my father's wedding ring. *What does that mean?* Nothing. I know for certain Dad often took it off before we did trips. Lots of people don't like rings pinching their fingers while rappelling down rope.

Her head reappears. "He said he was headed to the Lower Canyon for a few days," she whispers. "But he was —" Her voice trails off.

"He was what?" I prompt.

"— excited," she whispers, raising her hands to cover her eyes. "More excited than usual," she says even more softly. "And — secretive. I think he was ... hiding something from me."

"And he was going by himself?"

"Get out!" she screams at me. "Get out of here, this minute! Stop asking me these questions! Of course he was going by himself!" The sputtering words turn into a wail that frightens me.

I move to close the window, so the neighbours won't hear.

"I'm sorry, Mom," I say. "So very sorry." I grab the cup of water from beside the bed and offer it.

She bats it away, spilling some on the quilt, and stares at me through angry, watery eyes.

Better sad than mad. Did Dean really say that to me once? What did he mean?

"I'm leaving now, Mom. I appreciate your help. I promise I won't ask any more —"

"Out!" Her shaking hand points to the door, slightly ajar, where I can see Dean cowering. "But I forbid you from going into the Lower Canyon!"

• • •

"She hasn't told you everything," Dean says as I shut the door quietly behind me.

I freeze on the landing. "What did you just say?"

"Nothing." He runs down the stairs three at a time and all but knocks over furniture on the way out the front door.

By the time I reach the porch, he's sprinting up the driveway so fast that Elspeth's approaching moped veers into the overgrown hedge to avoid him.

"Dean! Dean!" she shouts. "Come back here, young man." But Dean has vanished.

"What did you do to make him run away like that?" she asks me.

"Nothing. Mom's wailing scared him."

Her foot delivers a healthy wallop to the moped's kickstand. She rises from her bike, removes her helmet, and shakes out her pink-streaked hair. "I see. And for what reason is your mother wailing?"

I'm about to say *none of your business*, when I remember that Elspeth is caretaking — if you can call subcontracting to Dean caretaking — for free. And me? I had let it happen by running around with Dominik. But the sight of the red napkin I thought was Dad's bandana has done something to me today. Made me certain, somehow, that there *is* something I need to find in the canyon. And that finding it will put our family back together, our reduced family of two.

Before questioning Mom, I had collected the address of the local Search and Rescue office, and that's where I'm headed next. So I've got to be nice to Elspeth a little longer.

"I tried to calm her. Maybe you can do better. Um, thanks for arranging Dean to help out." *I really said that?*

"You're welcome." Her jaw looks tight.

"Okay if I go out for an hour, or do you have to go home now?" My shoes are edging down the driveway.

"An hour's okay. No more than that if you want the meatloaf and apple pie tonight right out of the oven."

I force a smile to my face. "Thanks, Elspeth. Anything you need from town while I'm there?" Not that I have a dime to pay for anything, but it's a generous bluff, in my opinion.

"I'm good," she says as she hurries toward the house.

• • •

"I'm sorry for your loss, Tristan. And your mother's," says Major Dirks, the heavy-set man with a curlicue moustache who gestures me into his cramped office at Search and Rescue.

His face is weathered and kindly, and his Armed Forces uniform is full of badges that make him look important. The walls of his room are jammed with framed photos of him shaking hands with politicians, police officers, and rugged-looking teams of searchers.

"We assigned both rotary and fixed-wing aircraft to the search at the time, and made a considerable investment in officers and volunteers: trackers, canyoneers, and other highly experienced people. Your mother was fully co-operative, considering her understandably distraught state. And she accepted our conclusions when we finally called off the search. My files indicate you were included in our interviews. So pardon me for being curious as to the reason for this visit months later?"

I sit straight-backed in the chair across from his desk, place my hands neatly in my lap, and meet his eyes with all the confidence I can gather. "I was younger then, and too shocked and scared to even think of asking questions. But now, well, I can't help thinking about stuff. And since my mom doesn't want to talk about it, I thought maybe you'd help me."

"Do you have new information? Are you asking us to reopen the case?"

"No," I say quickly, leaning forward and placing my elbows on his desk. "Just a few simple questions."

"Okay, shoot," he says, failing to hide a frown.

"What was he wearing?"

Major Dirks opens up the file folder in front of him and lists off all the items my mother had named half an hour ago.

"Okay. And was he on his own or with anyone else?"

At this, the officer lets the file folder fall shut, folds his hands, and pushes his office chair away from his desk. He stares at the ceiling for a second, then looks at me sympathetically. "You're referring to the woman?"

"What woman?" My voice cracks.

"The woman canyoneer whose body washed up a few weeks after your dad entered the canyon."

My throat dry, I recall Harry and Angela's mention of the two incidents. I also remember reading and ignoring the news reports about the woman at the time. With my dad gone, I couldn't handle a story about the death of someone else — someone I'd never heard of.

"There was brief speculation in the press that they might have been connected, but we ruled it out. The woman, a geologist from Lillooet, was found many miles downstream weeks later."

"Geologist? Lillooet?" My brain takes a minute to make the connection. "Brigit's mother —"

The officer nods grimly. "Evelyn Dowling. Single mother of two. Our investigation concluded that she and your father did not know each other and were definitely not in the canyon at the same time."

"So, he was alone?"

"We believe so, yes. Your father's last anchor was found on Plunge Falls. As you know, we also found a few contents of his pack — his sleeping bag and a few clothes — floating just below Twin Falls, a little farther downstream. But not the pack itself."

"Oh." Again, that break in my voice. As my face goes warm, I recall now that they told Mom and me all this months ago, but I quickly blocked it from my mind. Somehow I needed to hear it again, now that I'm thinking more clearly. Who knows what Mom has ever told Elspeth.

Major Dirks attempts a sympathetic smile and he sighs as he looks at me. "As you know, we found webbing, anchors, and rope at various points down to Plunge Falls."

"Plunge Falls?" I hear the panic in my voice.

"I'm sorry, Tristan," he says. The major rolls his pencil between his palms. "His rope was frayed — chewed through by friction against the rock face of the falls, we presume — one hundred feet down. The falls is two hundred feet high, and there are boulders in the pool at the falls' base."

He stops and stares at the wall across from us. There's a long silence, like he's done. But I lean forward and wait, my fingers pressed on the edge of his desk, until he is forced to look at me again.

"There's no way of knowing how far he fell." He halts, then searches my face. "But something less than one hundred feet."

Another long pause as he shifts in his chair. "We assume he was killed … on the boulders below, and … well, the currents, log pileups, and so on kept … his body from reappearing."

I swallow hard. "Did you remove his rope?"

"My team left the anchors in place, but took the rope."

"And who was on your team?" Strange that I'd never even wondered that before, let alone thought to ask. It wasn't impossible I'd know someone. *Have I been in denial all this time? Unwilling, unable to contemplate the details? If so, why am I waking up now?*

"The canyoneering squad was led by Alex Carney, one of the most competent canyoneers in the area."

Yeah, right, I can't help thinking. *Except for being about profits over safety, according to Dad.*

"He and his team were in constant radio contact with our officers on the rim, in aircraft, and at the station."

He meets my silence with his own for a long minute.

"No further anchors or personal items were found," he continues more gently. "No signs at all much below Twin Falls. And despite our best efforts ..."

"Thank you, sir," is all I can force out.

"You're welcome, Tristan. I understand that sometimes knowing the facts puts family members' minds more at ease. We supplied you and your mother with the names of grief counsellors back when your father ... disappeared. If you would like that information again, I can ... It's especially advisable where there is ... no body —"

"— to grieve over. Thanks again for your time." And I'm out of there.

• • •

"You okay?" Elspeth asks as I sit fiddling with my fork over the steaming slice of apple pie.

"Uh-huh." I can't believe the woman whose body washed up in the canyon near the time of Dad's disappearance was Brigit's mother. *Why hadn't I put it together before?* She lost her mother last year, she learned canyoneering from her mother — and she has a chip on her shoulder. I feel sorry for her, I really do. But it doesn't mean I've warmed to her.

"Elspeth," I say as I pierce the apple pie slice and lift a morsel.

"Yes, dear."

"If I go into the Lower Canyon to see if there's anything else of Dad's that Search and Rescue missed … "

"Oh, Tristan! I'm so glad you've come around …"

" … will you look after Mom for the two or three days it'll take?"

She leans down and hugs me — a long, warm hug. For once, I let myself melt into her sympathetic touch.

"You know I will, Tristan. Of course I will. I'll handle your mother. And I trust you to be careful."

CHAPTER 11

"Hey, the Lower Canyon, no amateurs, and two overnights. This is going to be fun," Dominik says from the back seat of Alex's pickup truck, where my Polish friend and I sit with Dean sandwiched between us. Brigit is up front beside Alex, who's driving.

"You have to let me go, too. Why not?" demands Dean, kicking his sister's seat from behind, as Alex pulls the Chevy into the driveway of Brigit and Dean's run down bungalow.

"Not even a remote possibility, little guy," Alex says with an exaggerated laugh, prompting Dean to aim poison-dart eyes at his sister's boss.

"Dean, sweetie, I'm really sorry, but we've discussed it enough now," Brigit says in a firm voice, turning around and trying to pat her brother's head. Instead he arches back and kicks the seat again. "Someday I'll let you, honestly. Maybe in a few years. But it's a very serious piece of canyon, and you have to work up to it. Besides, this is an important mission, a search to help Tristan."

"I'm not getting out of this truck!" Dean declares, reaching to click the door lock. "And I'm not staying with that woman again! You can't make me!"

Alex chuckles like it's all an amusing game as he punches the control button that unlocks the pickup's doors, then jogs around to open the one needed to evict his employee's little brother.

"You're one determined boy, that's for sure. That'll work in your favour when you're a real canyoneer. But no small fry allowed on this trip, buddy. Besides, Elspeth is getting very fond of you. I think she's even taking you to a movie tonight."

"Like I'd be seen dead with her at the movies," Dean retorts.

It takes all my willpower to smother a smirk as I step out of the truck on the other side, but the smile vanishes from Alex's face.

He leans over, grabs Dean by his T-shirt, and says, "Out, kid. Brigit, can you please deal with this brat?"

"Dean! So good to see you," says Elspeth, gliding up the path in a tie-dyed T-shirt, shorts, and multi-coloured tights. "And look at all of you, a rugged team if ever I saw one."

She gives Alex a peck on the lips, which startles me. *Are they an item?* If so, my respect for Alex has just nose-dived.

Elspeth takes Brigit's hands in hers. "Don't you worry about a thing. He likes to put on a little act when you're leaving, but he's good as gold the rest of the time."

"Golden boy," Dominik teases Dean. "Behave, 'cause we're off. I promise to tell you all about it when we get back. And if Elspeth says you've been an upstanding young citizen, I'll teach you some tracking this weekend — assuming Big Sis allows."

"We'll see about that," Brigit says, enveloping her squirming brother in an extended hug.

"Tristan," Elspeth addresses me. "Good luck. Remember, channel your special powers of love and relationship, and you'll be successful."

I don't bother answering. I mean, *how could any self-respecting guy respond to that?*

"Okay, everyone. Running late," Alex declares. "Have to do a client pickup after I drop you all off. Can't believe I've given my best guide three days off. Just shows how generous I am." He winks at Elspeth and does some hand motions to usher us all back into the truck.

I feel half sorry for Dean, but sure don't want him on our trip. Wouldn't want to see him in the Lower Canyon anytime soon. I barely feel ready for it myself. He may be a feisty kid with amazing skills for his age, but he's still a kid. And a little jerk, given how he's half kicking Elspeth as she steers him into Brigit's bungalow.

• • •

Half an hour later, Alex pulls to a stop at the walk-in point.

"Tristan," he says. "A word with you alone, please."

Wary, I follow him a short distance away from Dominik and Brigit, who don't give us a second glance as they begin checking gear and chatting, even laughing. *Brigit actually laughs?*

Alex, usually so full of himself, is shuffling his feet and trying not to look at me. Then he starts in. "You know I was part of the Search and Rescue team that swept the canyon for your father."

"Uh-huh."

"Well, we did as thorough a job as we could, Tristan, buddy, but naturally we concentrated almost entirely on the creek and its banks. It's not like it was possible to check out every ledge or cave. So look up sometimes and —"

"I get it."

"Of course you do. Sorry, I know this is tough for you. Wish we'd found him alive, or even located his —"

"I appreciate what Search and Rescue did." It comes out a bit wooden. I want to smile and shrug like this is no big deal. But that would take a superhero, which I'm not.

"Did you know that Brigit was also part of the Search and Rescue effort?"

My heart stops. "Huh? She didn't even live around here then."

"Nope, she came down from Lillooet especially because I asked her to. I knew her from canyoneering up there sometimes. And she did fine; she's very competent and she worked hard. Anyway, I think it's nice of her to volunteer to help you out today. She didn't want Dominik along, wanted it to be just the two of you, but I figured a third person is always safer, and with Dominik's tracker skills —"

"Was it you who arranged for me to do the Upper Canyon for free last week?" I don't mean it to come out so bluntly, but the question has been bugging me.

"Um, yeah."

"Why?"

He looks down at his feet. "To see if you were ready for the Lower Canyon."

"Because?"

"Well, I'll just tell you straight, Tristan. Elspeth has been pressuring me for weeks to get you into the Lower Canyon. I don't know why she's convinced you'll find something all these months later, but when that woman gets an idea in her head — well, you know how women can be. And Brigit? I honestly don't know why she's so keen. She's not usually a fan of Elspeth's wacky ideas, but there you have it."

He lifts a hand and squeezes my shoulder. "Good luck, Tristan. And be careful."

• • •

Some time later, with that conversation still running through my mind, Dominik, Brigit, and I make it to the canyon rim. We ease off our packs, heavy with their extra load of sleeping bags and sleeping mats. My heart is doing double time, given it's my first ever trip into the Lower Canyon. There's also a heaviness to doing it against my mother's orders and leaving her yet again. Yet I hear the gorge calling me.

For a split second, I even imagine Dad materializing

from the trees and stepping forward to shake my hand. *You're doing the right thing, Tristan. You're ready for the Lower Canyon, and you need to do it for your mother. Also for yourself. You will find what you need, I promise.* The image disappears as fast as it played through my head. *Am I losing it?*

I try not to think of the way I left Mom: screaming, "No! Don't let him go!" to Uncle Ted, working herself into a real fit. I can hardly believe Uncle Ted encouraged me, and that he promised to stay with Mom while I'm away.

"I can tell you feel strongly about it, Tristan. Elspeth keeps insisting it will help Mary recover. So go ahead, but do be careful."

• • •

"Earth to Tristan."

"Uh-huh," I say to Dominik.

"We are ready to rappel."

"Oh. We are."

Brigit giggles and rolls her eyes at Dominik, who makes a face back. Come to think of it, they've been teasing each other like old pals the entire walk, while I've been kind of spaced out. *Hmm, flirting?* My Polish friend must be desperate to hit on a moody maniac like Brigit. Well, good luck to him.

"Hey, Brigit," I say, looking at the largest of the three backpacks on the ground in front of us. "I recognize your pack — just got those models in at the store last week."

"Guess I have good taste in where I shop," she says brightly, but she moves toward her bag protectively.

I reach for it and hoist it up. "Holy crap! This weighs a couple of tons. Are you training for Mount Everest or something?"

"I'm carrying the longest rope," she answers dryly, grabbing the pack away from me. "And the first-aid kit, dishes, and emergency gear."

"I was just kidding," I say, taken aback by how defensive she sounds.

"Wonder Woman," Dominik jokes. "Trying to show us all up. Okay, let us get suited up."

Right from the start, we're a tight team. We're all experienced, and not having beginners along keeps us moving fast and efficiently. Soon there's a rhythm to our actions. Brigit always tackles stuff first, while Dominik — who has the backup rope — is always last. Instructions don't have to be repeated or explained, and the jumps into clear pools become fun contests, which Dominik always wins with his signature double backflips.

• • •

By midday, we've already made our way down the first section; it's challenging without being death-defying.

"I calculate we have covered almost a quarter of a mile," Dominik says, studying his topographic map. "Not bad for a morning. If we put in the same effort this afternoon, we will be one-third of the way to our hike-out."

"We're doing great," Brigit agrees, "but let's take a break here." She disappears to scout ahead.

Lying full-length on a warm boulder, I hope she won't return soon. The morning has done great things for my confidence, but I'm sore and tired. All along the way, I've kept an eye out for sheltered ledges where Dad might have rested, and I've checked out half a dozen. My companions have indulged me in the extra time it takes, but really, we all know that this long after Dad's journey, it's highly unlikely there will be any trace other than the occasional anchor. We've found a few of those and left them untouched. *Shredded webbing won't help Mom.*

• • •

"Cool toboggan slide ahead," Brigit reports when she returns ten minutes later.

We rouse ourselves and position our bodies feet-downstream to slide down the chute. I enjoy the rump-bump and whoosh of the water on the way. As I bob up in the pool below, I catch sight of a cave-like formation in the granite ten feet above where we land. Brigit is staring at it. If she weren't, I might even have missed it.

"What do you think?" she asks.

"Worth a try," I say, and I allow Dominik to heave me up high enough to crawl into it.

Sitting at the entrance, I wait for my eyes to adjust to the dark. A thick cushion of moss blankets the little space, which smells moist and earthy.

"Channelling my special powers," I whisper as a joke. The carpet of moss absorbs my words. That's when I see the boot print.

Clear as anything: right in the middle of the tiny cave, like he's sitting here next to me. A perfect imprint of the left sole of his favourite canyoneering boots, the black ones missing from Mom's closet.

"You still up there, Tristano?" Dominik calls up minutes later.

But I want to be alone with the boot print, alone with what may be the only sign I'll find of my father on this trip. I want the imprint to tell me more — how he was feeling, whether he had any premonition, where things went wrong. Whether there's a ghost of a chance he's still alive.

"Tristan, you okay?" comes Brigit's voice.

I let my hands hover over the pressed moss as I fight back tears.

"Coming," I say a minute later, and Dominik's tall, strong body helps me down.

"A boot print," I say, choked up.

"And you think it might be his?" Dominik replies in a dubious tone.

"I *know* it's his," I say, perhaps too loudly.

CHAPTER 12

We're less than a quarter mile above Plunge Falls, according to our maps, although in canyoneering, that can mean an entire day's slog. The terrain has become steeper, more difficult, close to terrifying at times for me. I'm relying ever more heavily on Brigit's and Dominik's expertise.

"It's nearly dark," I alert my companions. "Don't we have to bivouac soon?" As in roll out our sleeping bags on a flat boulder or dirt patch.

Instead of answering, Dominik squats down at the base of a tree, then peers up it.

"What is it?" I ask.

"Baby warblers knocked out of their nest."

Brigit and I lean down to look. Three tiny feathered balls emit the faintest of squeaks. Their eyes blink as they lie barely moving on the ground.

"The mother has abandoned them," Brigit says in a gritty voice.

"Or she was rousted by a raven or eagle," Dominik suggests.

"We should leave them in case she can get back to them," I say lamely.

"They're goners, you idiot. Better to put them out of their misery," Brigit scoffs.

"No!" Dominik protests, looking at Brigit in surprise. "Let nature take its course. Whatever will happen, will happen."

"I'll tell you what went down and what will happen," Brigit says in a low and noxious tone, her face right in Dominik's. "A nasty predator lured the mother away, when she should have stuck to her chicks. Now they're paying the price."

As she looks up, we follow her gaze to a turkey vulture circling high in the sky. "See? That's their fate." And before we can move, she raises a boot, crunches the baby birds under her heel, and clomps off.

Dominik and I lock eyes. He shakes his head, shoulders his pack, and follows our leader. I turn away from the murdered birds and grit my teeth. My stomach has turned acidic; anger rockets up from nowhere.

"Brigit!" I shout.

She pauses but doesn't turn my way.

"I know your mom died in the canyon, and I'm sorry."

She spins around and stomps back to me. "Are you? What would you know about it? You still have one parent, useless as she is." Her bitterness hits me like spit.

"What did you say?" I shout. I have the urge to punch her.

"I said you still have one parent, even if she refuses to pull herself together 'cause she's a total wimp."

"Brigit," Dominik admonishes, lifting his hands to her shoulders and trying to steer her away.

She throws off his hands and glares at me. "It's your father's fault," Brigit declares. "If it weren't for him, my mother would still be alive. And I wouldn't be stuck raising Dean. It's not fair that I have to raise a kid at my age!"

Her voice has gone hysterical, and Dominik's face drains of colour as he watches us.

"What are you saying?" I demand. "Search and Rescue said they didn't know each other and were never in the canyon at the same time. My father was alone when the canyon killed him, if it even did. I know how it feels to lose a parent, Brigit. But blaming people who had nothing to do with it doesn't help."

My grief, buried deep inside me for months, is erupting in a spew of anger I didn't know I had. I'm fighting tears, Brigit is advancing on me, and Dominik is backing up with utter confusion on his face.

"You think they weren't together?" she demands. "Of course you think that, because I lied to Search and Rescue about the date my mother entered the canyon, and I lied about them not knowing each other. Why? To avoid the scandal. You should thank me. The truth is, she entered the same day as your father, *with* your father. I saw them leave together. And it wasn't the first time they'd hung out together."

"You're making it up!" I shout. "Shut up!"

"He lured her in. It's all his fault. What, you can't believe your father was a cheat and a liar? Ask your mom. She'll say she doesn't know, but women always do. Why else do you think she lies there all day, feeling sorry for herself? But don't cry to me about losing a parent and having to do a few more chores. You don't have a younger brother to raise on a tiny paycheque. Oh, look at you! You don't believe me, do you? So sorry to spoil your image of your perfect dad!"

She whirls around and takes long strides away from me. Dominik teeters on his feet as if trying to decide who to comfort. In the end, he gives me an apologetic look and skulks in the direction she has taken.

I sink to the ground, my emotions a toxic mix of anger, confusion, betrayal, and disbelief. First and foremost is the almost certain sense that her story is false. But there's also anger at my mother if it is true and she has known all along and has lied to me all these months. Anger at her unwillingness to deal with it, thereby making both my life and hers a misery. And then there's a dizzying rage at Brigit for daring to make all these accusations, which my heart tells me are not true. *Bullshit! Even if they were true, how dare she be the one to reveal them in such a heartless manner?*

For a second my eyes rest on the mangled baby birds; quickly I turn away. A thousand questions form, but two are more insistent than the rest: *Why did Brigit want to take this trip into the Lower Canyon? To "help" me? Nope. And why had she not wanted Dominik to come with us?*

I don't know how long I sit there on my own. I've lost all sense of time when I hear Dominik and Brigit

arguing about where to put their sleeping pads. *Fine.*
They haven't ventured far, but I refuse to join them.
All we brought for supper is sandwiches, anyway. I turn
my pack upside down and sort through everything that
falls out. I put my canyoneering gear to one side, eat my
sandwich, and spread out my mini sleeping pad, which
reaches only to my hips. Full-length ones are too bulky
and heavy for canyoneers to tote all the way down a
canyon. But by placing my empty pack beneath the rest
of me, I have sufficient paddling and protection from
the damp soil. I crawl into my sleeping bag and cry for
a long time, as quietly as possible.

CHAPTER 13

"Hot oatmeal!" Dominik's cheerful voice wakes me next morning. "Brigit put some extra brown sugar in it just for you."

I rub my eyes, struggle to remember where I am, and push my stiff body into a sitting position. Grogginess gives way to wariness as yesterday afternoon's exchange rushes back to me. I hold bitterness at bay as I wait to see how Brigit will approach me.

"We made a campfire." Dominik presses the steaming bowl into my hands. A spoon stands straight up in the centre. He's wearing a million-watt smile.

"Thanks!" I say, ravenously hungry despite bottled emotions.

"You'll need the energy." Brigit's voice drifts from where she moves to stand behind Dominik, her chin resting on his shoulder, hands around his waist. "We tackle Plunge Falls today."

I look at her, trying to determine her mood. *Is she not going to apologize? Will she take back what she said? Is she going to pretend nothing happened? And where does that leave me?*

"It's going to be warm and sunny all day," she adds perkily.

I narrow my eyes at her, waiting for something else. But she just smiles. "You were awesome yesterday, Tristan. I was impressed. Dominik was, too." She gives Dominik a hug. "And just as well, because it gets harder from here. Anyway, we should take our time after we do Plunge Falls, since there's more chance we'll find what you came looking for there."

Because the falls killed him, and his pack floated away, burst, and fed stuff into the current. That's what she thinks, but no one knows for sure where my dad drowned, if he even did. All Search and Rescue said was that they found his too-short rope dangling from the falls and no more webbing below that point, just his sleeping bag and some clothes not far downstream.

I suffer a flashback of Mom's and my conversation. She said Dad was unusually excited about the expedition. And it clearly upset her that he'd left his wedding ring behind; she seemed to believe he was keeping something from her.

No! I refuse to believe it!

To push those thoughts away, I study Brigit's profile as she stands with her back to me, studying the canyon section downstream. *Where does she think her mother was killed? And is that why she talked her way onto the Search and Rescue team looking for my dad, to find remnants of her mother while pretending to look for my father?* I'd never dare ask her. And anyway, my stomach is too empty to deal with such dark thoughts right now.

After I've gulped down my breakfast, crawled into my damp wetsuit, and stuffed things into my pack, we're off. As always, Brigit is leading, Dominik behind me.

"You have twisted taste in girlfriends," I whisper to him when she's out of earshot.

He grins. "I like complicated women. They are more interesting." His face turns serious. "But cut her some slack for last night, Tristan. She is hurting just like you are. Just shows it a different way."

"Yeah, mad instead of sad." I refuse to contemplate her words about my father and her mother. Made up because she needs to blame someone. Her mother's death left her a difficult life, for sure, especially with no father in the picture. Maybe I'd be bitter enough to concoct stories, too, if I were her.

She's right about the gorge getting more difficult. The walls narrow, and the water turns deeper and swifter. I breathe in the earthy smell of moss and enjoy its electric green glow on surrounding boulders. Sometimes the stream fills the entire floor between the canyon sides, forcing us to drag ourselves through knee-deep water. Other times it turns into pools so deep we have to float on our packs, chest-down and turtle-like, splashing happily like kids in a summer pool.

Twice, Brigit swims diagonally across the stream with a rope to set up a traverse line that we cling to in order to cross a treacherous current to a safer route. Even if I'm pissed at her, I have to admit that she has strong canyoneering skills. At regular intervals, we scramble over brush, dirt, and loose rocks on ledges above the water. There, we loosen the straps on our packs, so that if we fall in without time to shed them, we can struggle out underwater before being caught in debris or swept over a falls.

"What's this?" I ask at one point, staring ahead at a gigantic tube of rock that is funnelling the water into unknown darkness. It resembles the body of an airplane that crashed nose-down and rests, like the plunging stream bed, at a thirty-degree angle; it's channelling the entire creek through it like a tilted culvert. And there's no way around either side of it without climbing up massive rock slabs.

"Let me lead here," Dominik suggests, digging his headlamp out of his pack.

"Sure," Brigit says with a shrug. "It looks more dangerous than it is. It's really kid stuff."

After anchoring our rope around a secure boulder that resembles the plane's "tail," Dominik enters the giant tube slowly and cautiously, peeking out the occasional porthole-sized "window" as he goes. If it were a real plane, it would surely rank as one of the largest aircrafts around. The question is: *What lies in the dark, wet cockpit ahead?* Of course, Brigit wouldn't let Dominik enter if she weren't certain of his ability to retrace the route with the ascender (a mechanical device that lets you go up a rope), should things dead-end in a blockade of rocks or logs. Still, blind corners and stream beds that convert to caves or tunnels are nerve-wracking.

Minutes later, Brigit nods as we hear a long whistle from Dominik: the all-clear signal. Switching on my headlamp, I take the rope Brigit hands me and prepare to rappel down the slanted rock aisle. But as always, I double-check that it's the correct rope strand, the one that allows me to brake at chosen intervals, rather than slide to my death.

My heart seizes up when I realize I'm holding the wrong one. "You trying to kill me?" I say, shocked.

"Just testing you," she says with an evasive smile.

Huh? What game is she playing? I hesitate before I take the rope and enter the "plane," backing down feet-first along its flooded central aisle, working my friction device on the rope to control the speed of my descent. Soon daylight disappears, and I'm in a wide, dark cave — *the first-class section after lights out,* I tell myself for fun. The black, frigid water that reaches to my calves chills me; the cacophony it makes as it rushes ahead reverberates like a crowd of panicked passengers.

"Let me out," I say, shivering as rocks beneath the water tear at my boots, knees, and gloves, and spooked as my headlamp reveals moist walls, mud-caked boulders, and shadows that seem to be moving.

A second later, I see two things at the same time: light bursting through a slot where the water pours out below me, and a red bandana tied to a spire of rock along the right wall.

Resisting the current and ignoring the piles of rocks in my way, I manoeuvre my rope to clamber toward the sun-faded red cloth and reach out. Just shy of touching it, I feel a rush of mixed emotions: both heavy-heartedness and cautious joy.

So Dad passed through here last fall. He probably didn't mean to, but he left me a souvenir, a sign. *Dad, I'm tracking you. Where are you hiding? Let's not play this game anymore.*

It's tied tightly, and I'm at the limit of the rope clipped into my harness, but I'm not leaving this item behind. I pull off my gloves and let my stiff, ravaged fingers untie the bandana. I examine it reverently and see his initials in permanent-ink marker in the corner. His handwriting, his bandana. I stick it down my wetsuit, put my gloves back on, and return to the water flow.

In the unlikely event of a water landing, please proceed calmly to the nearest emergency exit. Inflatable slides will deploy automatically. My imagination keeps me moving toward that plane-nose exit without panic.

I smile with relief when I spot Dominik standing shoulder-deep in a pretty pool below, waiting for me to pop out of the cockpit-turned-faucet, which spills water six feet down into crystalline blue.

I unhitch my pack, shove it over the lip, peer down at the clear azure, then execute a cannonball sure to soak my friend.

"Hey!" he mock-complains.

"Amazing!" I say as I grab my floating pack.

"Kid stuff," Brigit repeats as she splashes down and nabs her pack.

"And look what I found inside," I say triumphantly as the three of us stand together in the sparkling water.

Got it, Mom. And then I hear the last voice I'd ever expect down here:

"Hey! Over here! About time you showed up!"

CHAPTER 14

I swing around and try to locate the voice. It's coming from beside the stream. Somewhere under a skirt of upside-down upper branches — the top of a giant tree that must have fallen all the way from the rim, spear-like, months earlier.

My eyes do a swift trip up to the forest and back. It's an Engelmann spruce whose upended roots are barely visible where they lean against the bank fifteen storeys above us. I shiver. Wouldn't have wanted to be standing here when that thing came down.

Of course, there's only one person who would have shimmied all the way down its trunk.

"Dean?" Brigit's face has gone stormy.

Dominik looks horrified. I'm not too thrilled myself.

"Hi, Brigit. I climbed down this tree after I hitch-hiked to the canyon!" He emerges from under the tent of green needles, grinning proudly, wearing a wetsuit, helmet, canyoneering boots, and backpack. But he doesn't seem in a rush to go near his sister.

"Dean Dowling! What the hell do you think you're up to? You can't be down here! And you're lucky you didn't kill yourself! Where is Elspeth?"

He shrugs, still beaming. "She's easy to ditch."

"Did she leave you with Tristan's mom again?"

The smile fades and he turns my way. "No, Tristan's uncle took Tristan's mom to the hospital."

"What?" I ask.

"The nuthouse," he elaborates soberly.

"The what?" Brigit glances at me but without sympathy.

"Yeah, she had a nervous breakdown, the uncle said. After Tristan asked her a bunch o' questions 'bout his dad."

My body goes numb; I stare at our intruder to assess if he knows what he's saying.

"Sorry, Tristan," he says, hanging his head. "She's going to be okay, your uncle said."

"She — she —" I start.

"Yup, well, if you think you're joining our group, you're dead wrong," Brigit tells her brother. "If you came down that tree, you can go back up it."

Dominik's jaw drops. No one, not even Brigit, would send a kid up that near-vertical, 150-foot fallen tree, even if he had managed to make it down. Not without safety gear and a guide. And even that would be foolish, given that there's no predicting when the trunk might shift. She's bluffing, and Dean surely knows it.

Still trying to recover from the grenade just lobbed at me, I'm too paralyzed to speak.

Dean crosses his arms. "Can't make me. Anyway," he says, sliding his pack off his shoulders, "I brought a harness and carabiners, so I can do Plunge Falls with you." He jabs his thumb downstream.

"Dean —" Dominik says.

"Come here this instant!" Brigit orders.

"No," says her brother, shuffling backwards. "I'm staying no matter what you say."

"Brigit, if he's got a harness —" I'm about to say I'll take him home via the tree — however dangerous that might be — because I've got to get out of here, too. I've got to get to my mom.

"No!" Brigit stamps her foot and glares at her brother, which puts a pout on his face. Maybe she thought I was going to say Dean should be allowed to do the falls.

"Brigit," Dominik says, "it is safer for him to come with us until we hit a side canyon that you and he can hike up and out of to safety, than it is to send him back up that tree. Seems to me we do not have a choice."

She turns on Dominik with full wrath. "*Me?* You think I'm ruining *my* trip to haul him home? And leaving you and Tristan to finish the descent with no guide? *I don't think so.*"

I speak up. "But I don't want to finish it. I have to get home. I'll take him out."

In the silence that follows, I wade across the pool to where Dean stands, chewing on a piece of licorice, a wary look on his face.

"Dean, why did you climb down that tree?" I ask, even though it seems a dumb question.

He hands me a piece of licorice like it's some kind of peace offering. I stuff it deep in a pocket. Then he leans in and whispers, "To look after her. And you."

"Huh?"

"Have to tell you somethin', Tristan. You know my sister cycles?"

"Of course. I've seen her mountain bike a couple of times —"

"Stop whispering, you two!" Brigit orders, even more incensed.

The three of us argue over Dean's head for a good ten minutes, but in the end, it's inevitable. The tree climb is ruled too dangerous.

For the next two hours, our new foursome trudges through the creek, slides down slippery chutes, and lowers itself over rock piles in mostly tense silence. Dean manages to keep pace and out of trouble. And Brigit puts considerable effort into keeping him and me apart, unless I'm imagining that.

It's late afternoon by the time the roar reaches our ears. There's no mistaking the horizon line, the soft mist that rises and wets our faces, or the powerful throb of the two-hundred-foot cascade.

"Old anchor," Brigit declares as she points to a tattered, faded loop of webbing around a downed tree lying between two large rocks. I suck in my breath. My father always used tan webbing to minimize visual impact on the environment. This one is tan. It's my father's: the last one he placed before the rope attached to it failed him. At least, according to Search and Rescue.

I picture Dad rappelling down, water flow pounding him in such a way that it bounces him around on the rope, which saws against a sharp rock sticking out of the falls' rock face. Search and Rescue said his rope got sawed through at the one-hundred-foot mark, so he fell way less than that; it takes a while for a rock to cut through rope, and the pressure wouldn't have started till he was well under the sharp bit. He could've fallen thirty feet or less. Survivable if he didn't hit rocks. Maybe even survivable if he did.

All day we've inched along beneath sheer, towering walls. There has been no possible exit. Tackling two-hundred-foot Plunge Falls was Dad's only option, even if he was short of a backup rope. He took his chances and carried on down. That's what canyoneering is all about.

I turn to see Brigit, Dominik, and Dean staring at me.

"You okay?" Brigit asks.

"Uh-huh." *Her mother may have lost her life here, too,* I remind myself. "Are *you* okay?"

She frowns and turns to push and kick a boulder, testing it for solidity.

"It's not going anywhere," Dean says.

"Perfect anchor," Dominik rules.

"Better than that tree," Brigit adds.

It's not the tree anchor that failed him, I want to say. *It was the rope and the sharp rock.* I understand that today, using a different place to anchor is all about separating ourselves from bad luck and negative energy. And yet, a part of me wants to wade out to the log and touch that last anchor, hold it to my lips for just a second — or rip it from the felled tree and sling it down the falls with an angry yell.

"On rappel," Brigit is saying, her harness attached to the rope, her hands and feet ready to work her descent. "On this one, when you get midway down the falls, you have to traverse left to avoid the main blast of water."

"Got it," Dominik says soberly. "Everyone hear that?"

We nod.

As she disappears over the lip, feet presumably moving through the lightest flume, helmet bobbing until it's out of sight, I release my breath. I didn't even know I'd been holding it. My hands and feet are prickling, all pins and needles.

"You are next," says Dominik.

"You'll be okay." Dean tries to assure me.

I look at him, galled that he, a kid, would dare to try and reassure me. "Have you been spying on us from the rim?"

"Of course. Waiting to find a tree I could climb down."

"And on our other trip, the one with those two clients? You were up there watching us, too?"

"No." He crosses his arms over his chest.

"What about that day Dominik and I went tracking? Did you follow us, maybe kick some rocks on me from up top?"

"No! Stop accusing me of things! I wouldn't kick rocks on you," he says, face contorted like he's genuinely offended.

"Sorry." I sigh, clip in, and move to the falls. "On rappel."

"Go easy, and keep out of the flow as much as you can," Dominik advises, as if I don't know that.

I've rappelled down falls before. I've been pummelled like I've stuck my face in a burst fire hydrant. But this one — it's overpowering, even in the lightest train of flow. It threatens to tear my pack, boots, and face right off. It bounces me around — and I stare warily at the razor-sharp rock sticking out mid-cliff beside the falls. With all the determination I have in me, I keep my feet on the wall and both hands on the rope, except when I've got to lift one momentarily to keep myself from hitting the wall. I sense, more than see, where I have to traverse left to avoid being torn to shreds — where a five-fire-hydrant blast will make a continuing safe descent impossible.

It seems like hours. My skin feels puckered beyond raw, and my hands are shaking, but finally I see Brigit through the mist below me. She's standing on a wet rock island that extends under the falls. She's pointing to where she wants me to land. *Was it Dad's landing spot, too?* Teeth gritted, I lower my boots onto the wet rock and let go of the rope.

Brigit moves toward me, I presume to help me downstream, so I don't slip into the under-falls whirlpool. Instead, loud enough that I can hear her above the falls' noise, she hisses in my ear, "Did you put Dean up to it? Did you encourage him to follow us? Is this your fault?"

"Don't be stupid, Brigit. Why would I want your brother here messing up our trip? I'm not *that* fond of him, sorry to say. Now let's move, so Dean can land safely."

Instead of moving clear, she reaches for the rope from which I've just unclipped. "If I pull it, they can't come down," she says, shouting in my ear as the falls thunders around us. "We'll be rid of both of them. They'll find a way out."

Huh? No freakin' way she's going to pull that rope on my watch.

She has the bottom of the rope in her hand. Her pupils look ready to pop out. I don't believe she's going to do it, but before I can form a thought, I push her off the rock into the frothy water. I push her downstream of the island, away from the dangerous currents directly under the falls, so she's not likely to get sucked down and drown. She'll just be wet and pissed off.

• • •

A few hours later, darkness is falling as the four of us spread out our pads and sleeping bags. It's a relief to see that Dean brought one of each for himself. Brigit, who hasn't spoken a word to me since I pushed her into the water, seems to have a quiet, contrite Dean on an invisible leash. He doesn't leave her side and displays none of his usual spunk or humour. She sets up their camp on a flat boulder a stone's throw from Dominik's and my dirt bench.

Brigit has ignored Dominik from the minute he completed Plunge Falls behind Dean, and his long face makes me wonder if she's blaming him, too, for somehow encouraging Dean to follow and drop down to us.

Since no one is offering to start supper, I move toward Brigit's pack to retrieve the grub.

"Don't you touch it," she commands in a poisonous-sounding voice.

"I will organize supper," Dominik offers, heading to her boulder.

Brigit opens up her pack, hands him the food bag, then closes the big bag with a loud click of the buckles. Shoving it behind her back, she rests on it like it's a sofa cushion, one to which no one but she has access.

When his sister's back is turned, Dean catches my eye and jerks his head ever so slightly toward her fat pack.

He's trying to tell me something, but there's no point attempting to interpret it. I'm not going to do anything more to annoy our guide — whose mood is like that of a grizzly bear with a toothache — than I already have.

Dominik slices up some salami, cheese, and bread, adds squares of a chocolate bar for dessert, and hands it around. The water beside us burbles noisily. Mosquitoes appear and whine in our ears. None of us has bothered to bring repellent, given how often the stream would wash it off in a day. The sun sinks in a pink and orange haze as shadows take over our camp. Crickets begin singing their nightly tune to our tense, silent gathering.

"What is happening tomorrow?" Dominik finally asks.

"I'm contemplating our options. I'll let you know in the morning," Brigit says curtly.

CHAPTER 15

The buzz of insects forces me to raise one eyelid. The sky tells me it's morning and an overcast day. Squeezing my eyelids shut again, I picture Mom in the hospital. Guilt and worry flood me; I want to leap up and go to her. Instead, I replay yesterday's strange events in my mind, then roll to my right to see if Dominik is awake.

He's gone. No Dominik, no sleeping bag, no pack. Probably he rose early to track some unsuspecting creature.

I roll over the other way to ask Brigit and Dean where he's gone. Their boulder is empty. No sign of anyone. Nothing left behind.

What? I jump up and at high speed, pull on my wetsuit and stuff things into my pack.

"Brigit? Dominik? Dean?" I call out.

There's a faint echo from the granite face across the stream.

My pulse runs riot. *They wouldn't abandon me. They're just ahead scouting or something.* I crouch down to check their trail. There's a muddle of boot prints where they converged and started downstream along the bank, clearly walking slowly and silently so as not to wake me up.

Then I see a boot print upstream of theirs, one that doesn't belong to our group. It's one solitary print beside where I slept.

I lean down to sniff, touch and analyze it. It's fresh, no more than a few hours old. My heart convulses. Joy, disbelief, and confusion all flood my senses. By leaning in even lower, I confirm by 150 percent that it's Dad's boot: his and no one else's.

And it's from last night, no doubt about that either. Dominik would surely confirm my conclusions if he were here.

"Dad?" I shout. "Dad? It's Tristan! Are you here? Are you okay?"

The echo mocks me.

Despite my best tracking skills, I find zero other signs of my father, not even the faintest trail indicating where he appeared from or carried on to. *Nothing, nil, nada.* Like I'm a total dickhead instead of one of the best hound dogs around. There's only one explanation: He was at my side at some point in the night, and wants me to see he was here, but doesn't want me to track him farther. He has the skills to do exactly that.

But why has everyone left me this morning? Eventually I'm forced to leave camp and follow my group's trail.

Phew! I'm relieved when I see Brigit ambling toward me.

"Tristan! You're up! Figured you needed some extra sleep," she greets me. She extends cupped hands filled with wild salmonberries. "Hungry?"

"As a wolf in winter. Where are the others?" Damned if I'm going reveal the panic I had earlier, or the visit from Dad.

She pushes past me to spill her load of berries into two bowls arranged on a flat boulder beside her pack and digs out two spoons. "I talked Dominik into taking Dean up and out. We found a safe spot. So it's just you and me now."

"You talked —"

"You heard me. They're hiking out. They've got the ascender device, pulley, and backup rope, and Dean's in good hands. He didn't want to go, but he had his fun yesterday. Even managed to do the falls. Did pretty well, considering." She sounds cheerful, proud, a different human being from yesterday.

"And Dominik was okay with babysitting him up to the top? Then Alex will pick Dean up or something?"

She chuckles as she sprinkles sugar on the berries. "Exactly. And I promised Dominik he could drop down and rejoin us before the end, while Alex and Elspeth put Dean into lock-up."

"Lock-up?"

"I'm joking. But Elspeth has to find a way to keep him from returning, or she'll be in deep, deep trouble with me." There's a sour, scary undertone in her voice.

"Uh-huh." I try to imagine how Brigit talked Dominik into the task. I imagine her cozying up to him and pouring on the charm just long enough to get what she wanted. Polish passion clearly fries the brain circuits. The bigger worry is whether she has some kind of new agenda now that it's just her and me. I want to search for Dad, now that I've seen signs of him, but I also want to get away from Brigit and get back to Mom, if she's in the hospital. I'm torn, but am determined not to let Brigit see that.

"Brigit, you know I have the bandana, and I don't really need to carry on to the bottom of the Lower Canyon. My mom's in the hospital, and I'm sure Uncle Ted needs me. The shop's losing money. I've got to start working. I can't just carry on like I'm on vacation."

Is Dad really alive? He'll show himself again if he wants to, or maybe he'll follow me home. He'd want me to get back to Mom, for sure. Anyway, I can search for him once Brigit is out of the picture, right?

She tilts her head and surveys me with that same smile, the one that now makes me suspicious. "Sure you can carry on. Your mom's in good hands. Better off than she was before, since she can't pull it together on her own. And you don't want to wimp out on the very last part of the Lower Canyon. Not after wanting to do it all this time. And by the way, Alex has made a generous offer to your uncle to buy the shop. "

My eyes narrow. Firecrackers erupt in my chest. "Alex has no right to go behind my back like that! Uncle Ted would never sell without talking to me. And you don't know anything about me or my mom! You don't give a shit about either of us, and who says I've always wanted to do the stupid Lower Canyon?" My raised voice startles some starlings from a nearby bush.

You're letting her get to you, Tristan. Embrace calm. You're supposed to stay strong and positive.

No! I'm sick of being Mr. Strong and Mr. Positive!

She keeps the smile on her face. "It'll all sort out when you get back, Tristan. Relax."

Relax? Is she for real? But a question pushes itself forward and overrides all the other crap for now.

"Brigit, do you think my dad might still be alive?"

Her smile grows larger. "I know he's alive, Tristan."

Electrical charges travel down my spine. "What? Why wouldn't you have told me before? As if you'd know, anyway."

"Tristan, chill," she says in a too-calm voice. "He ran off with my mother. They were hiding out together. He wouldn't want you or your mom to know that, would he?"

"You're a freaking liar, Brigit. You make up ridiculous stories and think I'll believe them."

She shrugs. "I couldn't tell you in front of Dominik or anything, but when I was on the Search and Rescue team looking for your father, he approached me when no one else was around. At Twin Falls, which is still downstream of us."

My entire body goes rigid. My vocal cords shut down.

"He wanted to know if my mom had made it out. He told me they faked their death at Plunge Falls, so they could take off and be together, but then she disappeared on him. He was searching for her and hiding from Search and Rescue."

"You think I believe a thing you're saying? You're the one who needs a mental ward!" I spout. "He wouldn't even know who you are!"

She sighs and looks at me with something like pity. "He knows who I am. He was at our house in Lillooet."

I pretend to play along for a minute, to see what other crazy shit she's going to serve up. "And what did he say when you told him your mother had drowned?"

"I didn't."

"You what?"

"I told him she was still in the canyon looking for him. So that he'd keep suffering. So that he'd die down here searching for her, since it was his fault she'd been lured away and died in the first place."

Goosebumps have broken out all over my body. I would declare her totally insane except for one thing: I saw my father's boot print. "And you never told Search and Rescue you talked to him, that he was alive?"

She shakes her head with an air of satisfaction. "Nor anyone else until I told you just now. But I know he has been watching us the last few days, Tristan. Maybe following us. You feel it, too, don't you?"

I shiver despite myself. "If Dad were still alive, he'd have come home," I declare. "And if he were here now, he'd come talk to me."

"Would he, if he is still looking for my mother and not wanting you to know that?"

Still looking for her mother months later? Seriously? Brigit is nuts! I grit my teeth and refuse to answer. She looks pleased with herself, like she has won a round or something.

Peering about, I weigh my options. Brigit has the main rope and best gear and knows how to carry on down the canyon. I've got to stay on her good side until I can escape, especially since Dominik has taken most of our spare equipment. But escape I will, and as soon as I can, because the woman is scary dangerous.

"So, ready to move on down? Some fun stuff ahead."

"Um, what about breakfast?"

"Um, ya! Coming up, Tristano. Fresh wild salmon-berries, sweetened."

CHAPTER 16

The rain starts pelting while we're eating. I spoon down the salmonberries in a hurry.

"Could flash flood, Brigit. We should climb higher, in case."

"Nah. Just a little local precipitation. Let's do a rappel or two and then decide."

She selects a stump to serve as an anchor and prepares to shimmy down to the next stretch, twelve feet below. "If I signal you to jump, go for it."

"Okay."

A minute later, I peer down and hear her blow the all-clear signal on her whistle. I also see a white shadow lurking under the water, like a granite boulder that could shatter my body. I toss my pack down and opt for the rappel.

"Could've missed that by a mile," she says when I point it out. But I'm trusting her less and less.

"How far away is the feeder canyon that Dominik and Dean took?" I ask.

"Around the next bend."

I relax a little. She may not know it, but that's my exit ramp, where I'll be leaving her Horror Show Swallow Canyon Expeditions tour, now down to just one non-paying customer.

Meanwhile, the stream section through which we're slogging in the ever-steadier rainfall has risen to thigh-chilling deep. I peer up and see a ledge five feet above us that would make things safer and easier. A skinny overhang, for sure, but I'd rather make like a tightrope walker than half swim in rising, waist-deep current.

Moving to the stream's edge, I balance on a wet rock and reach my fingertips to the ledge. It takes several tries, but eventually my bouldering experience and upper body strength gets me up there, pack and all.

Brigit watches with a frown, then moves reluctantly to the same stone. In attempting to pull herself up, she slips and falls into the stream.

"You okay? Your pack's too heavy," I say as she clambers to her feet. "Hand it to me, and then I'll pull you up."

"No!" she snaps.

No? What's with her precious pack that makes her all but cling to it? Instead, with admirable determination, she tries several more times until she manages to join me.

With our backs to the wall, hands feeling along it for balance and packs hanging off our shoulders, we glide sideways like nervous crabs, fingers pinching whatever knobs the granite offers. I'm having an easier time of it, since Brigit's bulkier bag forces her farther out from the wall. It doesn't help that the rain is now battering full force and the ledge is slippery.

• • •

Suddenly, Brigit totters and screams as she falls into the water.

I watch, horrified, as she thrashes about under the fast-moving water, trying to escape from the pack she had not fully lowered from her shoulder. Time slows as I witness her struggle in watery silhouette. I'm about to shed my own pack and dive in, when she surfaces, gasping.

Her pack pops up beside her, and she reaches for it to help keep her afloat, but it slips from her grasp as the current hurls her toward a narrow drop-off. She has just enough time to aim her feet downstream before she disappears. A second later, her bag lodges itself solidly across the chute.

Uh-oh. That's not going to be easy to get. But I'm on it. I break off the end of a branch sticking out from the wall beside me and squat down to poke and prod the pack in an effort to coax it down the slide. No luck. I grab my throw-bag rope and locate an upward-thrusting bit of stone in the wall beside me that allows me to hang off my ledge and reach down to attach the other end of the rope to the backpack. Five minutes of grunting later, I finally manage to haul Brigit's runaway pack up beside me.

I lift my whistle and offer a long blast to let her know I'm okay.

I hear a faint whistle indicating she's okay, too.

"Got your pack! Coming," I shout, even though it's highly unlikely she can hear me.

That's when I get a flashback of Dean tilting his head toward the pack. "Have to tell you somethin', Tristan," he'd confided, prompting his sister to order, "Stop whispering, you two!" And after that, she put lots of effort into keeping me away from both the pack and him.

Dean wanted me to open it.

I glance toward the chute. She has no way of seeing me right now. My gloves come off, and fumbling with wet, cold fingers, I unclasp the buckles and start digging. Rope, carabiners, and other metal gear, headlamp, food, first-aid kit. The usual. In another bag stuffed into the big one, her sleeping bag — but it feels strangely heavy and lumpy. My hand plunges into it, touches worn leather, fights to extract what is buried inside the bag.

A boot. Just one boot. The left-foot one.

My throat clamps up; my mind begins to race. Both times I saw Dad's boot print, it was the left foot. Never the right. And there was no further evidence, no trail, beyond the imprint itself.

She has been planting the boot prints for me, drawing me down the canyon for whatever perverted reason. My gut turns over with this devastating realization, and shivers travel down my limbs as I realize she's crazier than I imagined and *I am alone with her.*

Maybe she planted the bandana as well. But no — Dominik went ahead of both of us there. *Maybe she asked him to plant it? Could I trust either of them? Was meeting*

Dominik in the woods that day a coincidence or not? Had he already met Brigit? Why did he take off with Dean without even saying goodbye this morning, especially knowing I wanted to get out of the canyon to go see my mom?

I open my own bag to pull out the bandana. It's not where I stored it. In a panic, I paw through my pack. Someone has been in my bag and stolen it! The only trace I have of my father, the item that I'd hoped would somehow help my mother, is gone. It doesn't take much guessing as to who took it, but even when I remove every item in Brigit's bag, I've got to admit defeat. It's not in her pack either. *She tossed it away just to be cruel.*

Then again, I've been too eager to believe what I wanted to believe. I failed to stop and think logically. My father only ever wore his bandana on the approach to the canyon, not while actually canyoneering. It would have been in his backpack, not on his neck at the time he was in the place where I found it. And even if he'd gone to the trouble of taking it out and tying it to that spire in the airplane tunnel, Search and Rescue would have seen it months back. Come to think of it, floods would have ripped it away or frayed it until it looked much worse than it does now.

I don't know where she got hold of some of his stuff, but she must have been so desperate to make me think I was finding signs of my father, she didn't think things through — that he wouldn't have worn that bandana here in the canyon.

My father is neither alive nor following us. My entire body slumps and shrivels into itself with this realization.

The pain washes over me, hot and sharp, a cruel redo of the agony I suffered when we first lost him.

Where did she get my father's boot and bandana? Just forming the question churns my stomach. *And what else of his does she have from her Search and Rescue stint?* My body begins to shake uncontrollably. It's all I can do to remain standing on the ledge.

As rapidly as I can, I return everything to her pack, hopefully in the same order as it came out, and snap the buckles shut. I secure mine, too. Then I shuffle carefully along the ledge, my pack on my front, hers on my back, both hanging from just one strap down my shoulders, until I'm past the chute. I peer five feet down into a section of stream where my pale-faced guide is up to her neck in water, clinging to a bulge of rock.

I toss my throw-bag rope down to her and help her back up. We stand there a minute, shivering and clutching our packs, as the stream level continues to rise.

"That's where Dominik and my brother went," Brigit says through chattering teeth as she points downstream at a tributary streamlet coming in swollen with muddy water.

"Think they made it out before the worst of the downpour?" I ask. Somehow, I'm certain they did. I just wish I were with them. As I view the flooding channel, my spirits sink: *no longer an exit option for me.*

"They'll be okay," she says, but there's a hint of worry in her tone.

"And us?" I ask.

"We'll carry on in a minute." She forces a smile. "Maybe there will be a rainbow at the end of the rain shower."

"And a pot of gold," I say sarcastically.

She looks blandly at me. "My mom was a geologist, you know. She said there could be gold down here. It hides in gravel bars on the inside bends of creeks."

I snort. "Well, lots of bends on this creek, but I didn't bring a gold pan with me, did you?"

She gives me a half-hearted snarly look, then her shoulders slump with weariness. She opens her pack for a chocolate bar.

"I'm going a little way ahead to scout. I'll be right back," I say.

"No need to scout; I know what's coming up. I just need a few minutes to catch my breath."

"I know. Take what you need."

Ten feet, twenty feet, I'm finally out of her sight. The ledge goes around a corner and gets narrower, but I can handle it. *Think fast, Tristan. She'll follow soon.*

A patch of dense brush ahead and below is almost within jumping distance. As the ledge peters out, I edge toward those bushes. I lower myself to a crouch, but just as I'm ready to leap, the slippery ledge seems to slide out from under me. It plunges my flailing body, pack and all, into the water with a loud splash.

Water forces itself up my nose, and I wrestle hard to eject my pack. Gasping as my face emerges above the surface, I half swim, half crawl toward the bush, slippery rocks underfoot mocking my attempts to stand. I'm making headway, dragging my pack behind me, all focus on getting behind those branches, when I hear the shout.

"Tristan!"

She's standing there with a throw rope. *How did she catch up so fast?*

"Grab the rope! I've got you."

CHAPTER 17

We trudge on in silence, the rain easing. I'm in a lousy mood but trying not to show it. *Did she know I was trying to escape her? And why exactly am I in such a panic to ditch my guide, the one with all the equipment and knowledge of this place, anyway? Is it even right to leave her on her own, dangerous and deluded as she is?*

"Dominik will rejoin us soon," Brigit says cheerfully.

"Good," I say. *And hopefully not Dean, who is absolutely not up to this level of canyoneering.*

"The next big drop is called Twin Falls."

"Oh." I refuse to look at her; I pretend I don't remember her claim that she came across my father there during the Search and Rescue operation. She has a screw loose and a noxious nasty side to have made that up.

"Twin Falls is usually jumpable, but one of us needs to lower the other down just far enough to scout for where we should jump. In case a log has washed in or rocks have shifted during spring melt."

"Makes sense. I'll scout if you like." *Then I'll let you jump, but I won't jump after you.*

At this point, big drops are like burned bridges to me. Not since Plunge Falls have we scrambled down anything impossible for me to make my way back up. I should know; I've been memorizing the route like a Special Forces agent on reconnaissance. But if I jump down Twin Falls — which she just described as a big drop — my fate will be sealed. I'll have to carry on to the end of the canyon with this madwoman pretending to believe my father is wandering around the canyon somewhere, searching for her drowned mother.

Alex told me Brigit wanted to do this canyon alone with me. And here we are, just the two of us. Why? The very question spooks me.

"She cycles," Dean had told me like he was confiding some big secret. *What was he trying to say?* Cycles, cycles, cycles. I think again how crazy Brigit seems, then it strikes me: Her brother wasn't informing me that Brigit rides a bicycle. *Duh.* He was trying to tell me she has phases. The moon has lunar phases, or a cycle. And there's a reason they call crazy people lunatics. *Right? So, maybe Brigit seems normal for a while, then turns into some kind of maniac, then returns to calm and logical.* I can totally believe that.

Another thought comes to me. When I asked Dean why he'd slid down that tree, he replied, "To look after her. And you."

And me? To protect me from her?

With neither Dean nor Dominik around anymore, I've got to protect myself. And that means getting out of here. After Brigit jumps Twin Falls, I will turn and make my way back upstream to that exit that Dominik and Dean took earlier. And wait an hour or two or whatever it takes for the water level to drop.

A low-throated rumble brings me back to the present. Waterfall ahead.

"Here it is!" Brigit says.

I force a smile and nod. A fog floats above Twin Falls like a phantom. I shiver despite myself. *Maybe Dad did survive Plunge Falls and managed to find shelter somewhere around here? No! He'd have made his way home. Don't believe Brigit's lies.*

But I have nothing to bring home to Mom. Not even the bandana. Well, a left boot if I raid Brigit's pack for it. But neither boot nor bandana are really going to cure my mom. That thought drop kicks into my brain for the first time. I'm on this mission because of Elspeth, the town hippie. Elspeth means well, but my mom needs real help. The kind she's probably getting now in the hospital. I'm worried sick about her and I miss her. With my dad gone, she's all I've got. It's time to get home.

• • •

I crash into Brigit when she stops just upstream of the drop.

"Hey! Watch where you're going," she says.

"Sorry."

The canyon walls curve in on either side of the falls, preventing us from scouting without hanging over the falls with rope. Three flat boulders ten feet back from the falls' lip resemble giant stepping stones that lead from the bank where we're standing to the middle of the falls. But they offer no undercuts, cracks, or edges for a safe anchor.

"Don't see anywhere to place webbing," I say worriedly.

"Never has been here," she says matter-of-factly. "We need to do a meat anchor."

She watches my face as I take that in. It means she's going to use her body to anchor me as she lowers me down. She's the "meat." *What does that make me? Dead meat? Ha ha. I'm really getting paranoid.*

"You said you'd do the scouting, Tristan. So I'm going to get myself to that middle rock and get ready for you."

"Uh-huh."

She leaps from stepping stone to stepping stone like she's on a casual stroll, not a few feet upstream of a drop-off emitting deafening thunder and clouds of spray. She sets up the rappel and sits straight-backed and cross-legged on the third rock like some kind of yoga master.

I follow, legs jittery as gelatin for no good reason. I grab the rope and clip in. If only I could see down to the pool below without being lowered down a ways.

The falls are swollen with the morning's rain shower, but there's a small gap in the middle immediately below our rock. A dry stripe between wide jet streams. Like long hair with a part in the centre. *Guess that's why it's called Twin Falls.* It's a gap I'll have to stay in to keep from being power-washed as I inspect what's below.

"Whistle three times when you want more rope," she says.

"I will," I say, lifting my whistle to my mouth and doing a little test. "Ready to be lowered."

Soon I'm in the stream and drifting toward the lip. That's when Brigit leans forward and shouts through the din of the falls, "This is where I met your father, remember? It's where he and I spoke. If he's still down there, *tell him to go to hell!*"

What? I grab for a rock to serve as my last-chance handhold, but it's too late. Brigit is feeding out the rope I'm on. My last glimpse of her is glowing eyes with over-large pupils and a smile that is pure evil.

I concentrate on staying within the all-too-narrow ribbon of oxygen between the falls' twin avalanches of water as I'm lowered. I look down. No logs, no pile of rocks in dead centre, but both to either side. The pool below looks deep.

Hardly has that thought registered when one accidental, panicky twist places me under one of the jet streams. Battered like a punching bag, I can hardly breathe or move.

Okay. I'm like a puppet on a string. I cannot climb up, and I need her to lower me out of this.

Screech! Screech! Screech! I blow my whistle with what breath I can find. It's a distress signal, though the last two blows sound like they're coming from underwater, more of a gurgle than a piercing call for help.

She has to have heard me; she knows. She can't be unaware that I need her to lower the rope. *She's letting me drown. But why? This is deliberate, revenge for her mother's death, right?* There's no help coming from above; it's up to me to take emergency measures. But I dare not release my grip on the rope until I'm out of the falls' force and hovering over the clear spot.

With all my strength, I push my left leg against the rock face. In response, the rope swings slightly to the right. If the falls doesn't drown me, there's a chance I can pendulum back to the clear centre strip, cut the rope, then fall. I'm much higher than I'd like for doing so, but better to take my chances dropping within the deep spot than to stay and drown where I am now. Which I will if she won't lower me down.

Two steps one side, two steps the other, ever closer to the air pocket "between" sections. Three steps one side, three steps the other — then I'm there. With a scream no one can hear, I slash the rope and fall through moist air and into a churning whirlpool that feels like it wants to suck me under forever.

Deep underwater now, I am like an astronaut without a tether, tumbling and pin-wheeling in suspended darkness, head over heels over head. Cushions of bubbles — so many bubbles — surround me like a bubble-wrap spacesuit. If I had no need to breathe ever again, I could spin softly like this forever, but already my lungs are crying out for release.

"If you're ever caught in a keeper whirlpool, dive for the bottom; the lower currents should release you downstream." *How many times did Dad tell me that? But what if you don't know top from bottom?* Yes, there are split seconds where my body is flung somewhere with pale yellow light that must be just beneath the water's surface. But never does the spinning force let me reach the surface for a gasp of breath. Instead, it yanks me viciously toward darker sets of bubbles, where I have no time to contemplate diving before being flung up again. *Must find a way out before my lungs explode.*

Unfolding my body as best I can, I flail my legs like a madman the next time it goes dark. And sure enough, some rogue current nabs me and kicks me like a football to somewhere that's not spinning.

When my head surfaces, I all but choke on the welcome air, then propel myself with every fibre of every muscle to a grey rock.

A rock means land. As I grasp its slippery sides, I feel I've been tossed to a different world. Slowly it dawns on me that I'm in a cave whose entrance is through twin walls of water. The current has thrown me not downstream but upstream. I'm behind the falls in a surprisingly large grotto. It offers a gravelly floor that tilts on one side into a giant mud puddle.

Brigit! She'll surely jump any second and propel herself in here to finish the job the jet stream failed to do. I have to hide, fast!

I gaze at the mud puddle, and hoping it's deep enough, decide it's what I need. I dig in my pocket for the stick of jumbo licorice Dean gave me and put it into my mouth like a cigarette. Breathing through the sweet, hollow stick, I sink into the mud and disappear from the world.

CHAPTER 18

Being submerged in a mud puddle doesn't allow me to see her stick her head behind the shower to do a quick visual of the cave. But I know when she does so by the muffled rant she conducts for a minute — no doubt directed at my father — and the gravel she kicks so hard that pieces plop into my puddle and rest on my chest.

I sense (or maybe just guess) when she exits, but even so, wait at the bottom for a very long time after she leaves.

When finally I rise and wipe brown muck from my face, I'm awed by my surroundings. Sun filters through the hydrosphere like a glass ball lighting a dance floor. I'm inside a miniature cathedral with a never-ending cascade of powerful music. Its ancient walls are pockmarked by a hundred cubbyholes, eerily like our grotto at home.

I stand and run my hand along the wet walls, poking my fingers into some of the niches. Instinctively, I look for the largest chink, in which rests a stone as big as a carved marble head.

My hand is drawn to it: the hand of my younger self seeking a prize as my parents gaze lovingly from nearby. Slowly, reverently, I roll the big stone aside, then step back in shock, certain I'm seeing a mirage. Standing there like a vase on a fancy bookshelf is my father's blue dented aluminum water bottle. Placed where only I would find it.

"You have powers they don't. I feel it in my bones, Tristan. Your ability to locate what he left behind." *How did Elspeth know? Maybe she's got more going on with her vibes than I thought.*

It takes me a full minute to work up the nerve to reach for it. I'm so afraid it will disappear before my eyes. When it's in my hands, I sink down to the cave floor and shake the container. Not a drop of water. I unscrew the cap, remove my gloves, and feel around inside. My fingers touch pages of a waterproof field notebook rolled up like a scroll. I pull them out, unfold them, and begin reading.

> *Dear Mary and Tristan,*
> *I hope you never see this letter, because if I make it home I intend one day to return and destroy it. I am holed up in the cave behind Twin Falls — the very cave that inspired me to design our grotto many years ago — with a broken ankle and cracked ribs. It is damp, cold, and lonely here, and I am beginning to succumb to hypothermia. I want to write you before help arrives or the canyon defeats me.*

Mary, my love, you know I was keeping a secret from you, but my only intent was to surprise you and Tristan with a wonderful gift — not to hurt you or allow fate to separate us.

Months ago I was approached by a geologist from Lillooet, Evelyn Dowling, who is convinced there are major gold veins in the Lower Canyon. She hoped to locate one so she could stake a claim.

Although a canyoneer herself, she wanted a skilled guide to accompany her, and offered me a percentage of the profits from the find if it materialized. We signed a contract accordingly. (You will find it in the smallest cavity of our grotto.)

We had to keep our discussions top secret, as anyone can pursue a gold find before it is staked, and there is no point registering it before actually taking the time to pan and assess it.

I'm sure I don't need to assure you, Mary, that there is nothing more than a business relationship between Evelyn and me. I state the obvious only because I suspect her somewhat unstable daughter, Brigit, believes otherwise, or that false rumours may spread if we do not return.

I know now I was a fool to keep the details of this trip from you, Mary and Tristan. I imagined announcing we were rich at the end of this descent. I suppose I caught "gold fever" from Evelyn.

The good news is that she was right. We found a significant lode, and should you get your hands on this note before anyone else, you and Evelyn's family can make money from it. (I've drawn a map below identifying the location.)

Now I will explain how I ended up in this cave. After Evelyn descended Plunge Falls without a problem, a sharp rock sawed through the rope as I was rappelling and dropped me onto the rocks at the bottom. I'm lucky to be alive. I broke only my left ankle. Evelyn helped me out of the water, but when I removed my boot to look at the injury, the boot slipped from my hands and disappeared downstream.

Despite our problems — including having lost most of our main rope — Evelyn and I managed to reach Twin Falls. There, while serving as a meat anchor for her, I had a shooting pain in my ankle that caused me to shift and tumble down. The fall broke my ribs. Evelyn insisted on carrying on alone to get me help. I had no choice but to agree.

So, as I write this, she is somewhere downstream attempting to complete the canyon. I worry whether she's up to the challenge, but God willing, she will succeed, and I will be home shortly.

If not, I'm comforted by having written this note. If I do not return, I beg your forgiveness. Mary, please be strong and help Tristan find his way in life. And son, know how proud I have always been of you. I know you will help your mother in every way you can.

Finally, if Evelyn does not make it out, I urge you to honour the contract and help her family.

My body is so chilled I'm shaking, and I'm overwhelmingly sleepy. I will stash this note now and crawl to where hopefully rescuers can find me.

With all my love, Julian

My sobs shake the cave until its walls, the world, and my heart crack and collapse.

Finally, balled up and fully spent, I lie immersed in muddy water and thought. Eventually, it occurs to me that Brigit found his boot near here; maybe she imagined seeing and talking with him. Maybe she just lied. No point dwelling on that. All that's important is that I get out of this damp place and back to my mom with this letter.

I wade through one edge of the water curtain and re-enter the world.

• • •

Canyoneering boots are more or less soundless. To make absolutely certain I've won my freedom at last, I move like the Sultan of Stealth I am. I've decided to follow Brigit at just the right distance behind. I'll trail her until Dominik appears, if he does and regardless of whether I can still trust him. I just hope that will be before a falls requiring more than my puny throw-bag rope. Meantime, I've got to find my backpack, which hopefully my crazy guide tossed down from her stepping stone.

The concentration and discipline of stalking Brigit soon gives me the buzz of total focus. I move like a tiger sneaking up on prey; all my senses are on overdrive. Brigit may be a canyoneer, but she's no tracker, and I know just how to stay unseen and keep from leaving any signs of my presence.

Judging from her boot prints, she's worried and in a hurry — perhaps concerned she didn't manage to kill me and I might be ahead. She has no idea how to avoid leaving broken twigs and upturned stones to flag her passage. In fact, it's like taxiing along a lit-up runway. Hours into the day, I note one point where she stops for quite a while, as if wondering if I might be following her. Another time, she tries hiding in a patch of high, wet weeds, but I can tell by the way the breeze passes over them where she is, and I remain still and hidden until she stands up and carries on.

Farther on, there's a muddy bend where it's clear Brigit has crouched down and examined the mud as if searching for my boot prints in case I'm ahead, rather than behind. But she's dealing with an experienced stalker; even if I'd snuck ahead, I'd never be caught unaware.

Bingo! I almost throw caution to the wind when I spot my pack, muddied and bobbing behind a log near shore. Again though, I sight signs of Brigit hiding nearby, perhaps thinking that if I'm still alive and following her, I'll show up here to claim it. Patience, my father taught me. *Slow down, clear your mind, make yourself invisible.*

Patience being my specialty, I wait her out for an hour. Only when I know she's well downstream do I emerge to grab it, open it, and cram a chocolate bar into my mouth, chased down by gulps of water from my bottle. Before snapping the pack's buckles shut, I stash my father's water bottle with its note inside.

• • •

The sun gets warmer; a breeze picks up and ripples the surface of the stream. The whole world smells like my mother's favourite air freshener. I figure it must be noon when I first realize I've seen no signs of Brigit for half an hour. None at all. *Wait! How could I lose her trail?* Until now, it has been as clear as footsteps pressed into wet cement. She can't just disappear. She has no idea how to be subtle. Unless — unless Dominik has rejoined her and wants to cover their trail. He would know how.

I find a stump, lower my ear to it, and listen for a long time. No people sounds. But the canyon around me has gone slightly quieter. *Hmm.* I scan the horizon left, right, and down. *Oh yeah, must remember to look up, too.* Just then, something drops from the tree overhead, knocks me over roughly, and headlocks me with a muscled arm.

"Ouch! Dominik! You're hurting me!" I'm flat on my back, kicking like crazy, rocks pressing into me.

"*Tak?* And why would I worry about that after you tried to kill my girlfriend? Think you are such a great tracker, do you? Think she is easy prey? Think again. Classic case of the hunter becoming the hunted."

"Huh? Dominik! Let go and I'll explain —"

"Like I would believe anything you say. You have obviously ditched her and are following her. And she already told me what happened on Twin Falls: how you would not pull her up or down when she got caught under the falls and whistled. She nearly drowned. What do you have against my woman? Canyoneering is dangerous enough without playing revenge games the minute I disappear."

Brigit moves into sight. Her smile is triumphant.

"Dominik!" I yell.

"So your father ran away with her mother. Who cares? Not worth turning against your guide, who had nothing to do with it. I never pegged you for a deranged creep, but you are not getting away with any more crap while I am around to protect her. Understand?"

I open my mouth, then close it again and exhale where I lie on the ground. *What's the point of fighting?* Dominik is no longer my friend. But one thought comforts me: *I don't think he'd allow Brigit to kill me in his presence.*

CHAPTER 19

We travel in tense silence for an hour before a rumble reaches our ears. *Uh-oh, a big drop.* I remind myself I was lucky not to bump into one while travelling alone and without a decent rope. There is an advantage to having rejoined my battalion, even if as a prisoner of war.

Defeated as I may feel in some ways, my body has not yet let go of the high-alert tracker mode I needed while avoiding Brigit. I remain hyper-aware of small birds hopping through leafy salal, the creak of branches stirred by the afternoon breeze, and the heat of the sun on my cheeks. So when we near the waterfall, I'm the first to see the ragged orange backpack beyond it, snagged on a dense bush growing out of a ledge halfway up the left side of the 150-foot-high gorge.

Glancing closer at the set of bushes where the pack has caught, I happen to spot the slightest movement: the wriggle of someone trying to stay still and hidden. Suspicions aroused, I run my eyes like high-power

binocs up and down the wall between rim and pack —
scanning dirt clumps, scraggly vegetation, and loose
rock for any signs that someone or something has recently travelled down that line.

By the time my companions pause and stare in surprise at the pack, I've already reconstructed the scenario.

"Where did that come from?" Dominik asks.

"Washed down and caught during spring flooding?"
Brigit guesses. She looks as startled by its presence as
Dominik does.

No way has Brigit planted this one.

"My dad's," I confirm. My words prompt both to
turn toward me.

"It obviously was not there when Search and Rescue
swept the place," Dominik says.

"Hmm," I agree, but my total concentration is
on the cliff, from rim to stream. The broken twigs,
spilled rocks, and traces in the dirt between the cliff
top and the hanging item indicate that someone relatively small — I'd bet a million dollars on Dean —
free-climbed down, hung the pack on the branch,
and is hiding this very minute on the ledge behind
the bushes.

Not with Elspeth's permission, that's for sure. He's a
second-time escapee, I'm betting. *Why would he do this?*
Just for the fun and challenge of it, knowing him. *Or
maybe he overheard Elspeth say something like the words she once
uttered to me: Darling, before your father disappeared, he must
have shed or dropped something. On a tree branch or ledge, perhaps. I feel it; I sense it.*

How did Dean get his hands on my father's pack? If Elspeth had had it all along, she'd have given it to me a week ago to help "cure" my mother, rather than encouraging me to go on some epic, dangerous search. Or just handed it to Mom herself.

No, my guess is that Brigit came across it — along with the boot — during her Search and Rescue expedition for my father, hid them in her pack, then in her house. She probably decided the boot and bandana were enough for her purposes on this trip, and left the pack behind.

I picture Dean stumbling onto the pack a day or two ago and cooking up the scheme of escaping Elspeth again and hiking through the forest to a point downstream of us to position it where we'd be sure to find it. Way more satisfying than waiting till I returned, or handing it over to Elspeth or Mom himself.

The scene is easy to imagine. Dean — enjoying his freedom in the woods and spying on us intermittently — chooses his spot and uses his considerable bouldering skills to scramble down the cliff to the bush on the ledge. *Why?* He wants a front-row seat to my retrieving the pack, and maybe he also wants to make sure all is well with his sister, Dominik, and me. *If he only knew. And ha!* Just now I catch a glimpse of his bushy black hair, though he's doing a helluva job staying still.

Will Dominik's sharp eyes spot Dean? Nope. He's too distracted by scouting the falls.

"Too marginal to jump, right, honey?"

"Correct," Brigit replies as she sets an anchor around a sturdy boulder and clips in. "Dominik, sweetie, okay if I go first and Tristan second? Then hold up a little while before you come down, please."

"Whatever you say," Dominik replies, beaming at her. "Then we will help Tristan get his father's pack?"

"If that's what he wants," she says, turning to me friendly-like.

Brigit completes her descent. I follow, landing lightly in the shallow water below the falls, beside her on the left side of the creek. There is precious little bank here, just the torrent tumbling steeply between the gorge's walls. Studying the pack hanging well downstream and halfway up the cliff on our left, I come to the same conclusion as Brigit.

"Impossible to reach without setting up a traverse line," she says. A traverse line is for crossing a more or less horizontal and/or upward diagonal stretch of wall that's too high off the ground to be safe for climbing without a rope.

"I'll free-climb up a ways and find a place to anchor in, if you want to do the traverse," she says.

That means I'll climb up to her and then take the lead away from her — toward the bush behind which Dean is hiding and where the pack is hanging.

"Okay." My eyes travel up to the backpack. *Where did you lose your pack, Dad? When you stumbled from exhaustion and cold from that cave and got dragged into the current? Mom will get better, Dad. I promise to look after her, like you asked.*

Brigit clambers ten feet up the gorge wall with our secondary rappel rope — slightly shortened by my earlier cut — which she got off Dominik before rappelling down the falls. The primary rappel rope is still dangling down the falls, of course.

She's clearly assuming I really want my father's pack. The truth is, I want a rope up there to rescue Dean; I'm worried about his safety. The bush he's behind is not well-rooted, and he probably has no safety line. Piles of jagged rocks lurk in the stream that's a seventy-five-foot freefall immediately under him. And unlike the portion of the wall he down-climbed, the lower half is sheer, smooth granite from the bush to the ground, no ledges or handholds to speak of.

Just because his climbing skills and guts allowed him to survive his dumb journey to the bush doesn't mean he can budge from there without help. *What was he thinking?* If Brigit knew her brother was present and in potential danger, she would freak. But I'm not about to reveal him yet.

A quick whistle blast sounds from behind. Dominik mimes the question of whether Brigit is ready for him to rappel down the falls and join us yet.

She holds up one finger: another minute. *Does she want him up there for safety reasons?* I wonder. *Maybe there's something downstream she hasn't told us about that makes her hesitant to have that rope pulled for good?* The creek certainly drops away fast and steeply below the falls.

"Tristan! Ready for you," she says.

She has herself and the rope anchored to webbing around an elbow of rock in the cliff face ten feet above me. She drops the rope my way. I tie the rope with a knot directly on the harness. Soon I've passed her and am lead-climbing, making my way upward and away from her along the cliff face, wedging my hands into cracks for handholds. It's nice to know that if I slip, Brigit and the anchor will limit my fall.

I've managed several dozen feet when I hear three whistle blasts from Dominik: the emergency signal. I turn and freeze. While I wasn't looking, Brigit unclipped herself from our webbing, down-climbed with no rope back to the base of the falls, and pulled Dominik's dangling rappel line, stranding him above the falls.

And having sprinted and free-climbed back up to the elbow of rock and clipped herself back in, she's ignoring Dominik's horrified look and attempts to shout and whistle at us. My eyes meet his, and I give him a flat stare: *It has taken you this long to figure out that she's dangerous?*

He'll find a way down. He may have no rope, but he can free-climb down slowly and carefully if he's desperate. He's a better free-climber than all of us. That, or I'll figure out a way to help him out when I return with Dean.

I pull my focus back to my footing. I'm tiptoeing along the edge of a poor excuse for a ledge, and handholds have all but disappeared. I'm still roughly at the same level as Brigit, but because the creekbed drops steeply in this section, I'm now a good twenty feet above the boulder-choked water. The nearly vertical stretch of granite beneath my toes features nasty-looking rocks beside the roaring whitewater.

I seem to be the only person aware that there's an all-too-smug kid behind the bush. Meanwhile, I'm being anchored by a psycho who's being shouted at by her jilted, puzzled, and momentarily helpless boyfriend.

At some point, either Dean is going to identify himself or Dominik is going to spot him and blow his cover. If either occurs before I'm within reach of Dean and get another anchor staked, Brigit will flip out.

My ledge is petering out; I'm in the most precarious part of my traverse. *Carry on for Dean's sake.* As my handholds and footholds become ever more sketchy, the pounding in my rib cage feels violent enough to toss me off the wall. Desperately I search the granite for anything to hold on to. I spot a large nose of rock halfway between me and the bush. If I can reach it safely, it offers a possible anchor site.

Three desperate whistle blasts all but rip off my ears. I look back long enough to see Dominik mouthing something at me and pointing at Brigit. The falls drown out whatever he is trying to say. *What now?* I look Brigit's way, and my heart chills. She has pulled her knife from the sheath on her harness and poised it above the rope anchoring me.

"Should I cut it or yank it?" she shouts at me.

My throat closes up. Cutting it may rob me of an anchor, but I'll still be safe if I don't lose my footing. If she yanks it, I'll be pitched off the wall onto the boulders below.

CHAPTER 20

The eyes she directs at me are those of a predator. And now I notice for the first time that she is no longer anchored to the webbing on the rock elbow. After down-climbing and sprinting over to pull Dominik's rope, she must have been so distracted or crazed that when she got back to her station, she accidentally clipped onto my rope instead.

She is inching along the ledge traverse toward me, putting herself in greater danger with every step. *She must think she's still anchored in.*

Drops of sweat drip from my forehead into my eyes. *Was I really so naive as to trust her and her elbow of rock as my anchor?* If she tugs on the rope, I plunge to certain death. And if I go, my rope will pull her down with me. Her body will hit the rock-strewn killer rapids with a force I don't even want to imagine.

Dean surely can see what's about to occur, but he hasn't moved an inch. Frozen with terror and indecision, he's no doubt aware that identifying himself now could as easily provoke her as stop her from committing a murder-suicide.

I size up the distance between my current position and the nose of rock ahead and above. It will require several minutes of tricky effort to reach, plus some webbing currently tucked away in the pack on my back to create an anchor called a "chockstone." If Brigit sees me pause and dig in my pack, I fear she'll turn suspicious and enraged. It'll trigger her to do the deed.

Both sweat and chills have taken over my body. *Is there anything I can do or say to persuade Brigit not to commit this crime?*

The tense stillness is broken by her shout. "I'm not trying to hurt you, Tristan. I just need you to be in danger so that your father will come save you. It's your father I want, not you."

That's comfort?

"But if he doesn't appear within five minutes, I will yank the rope." She waves her knife for effect. "Someone has to pay for my mother's death."

My heartbeat accelerates with the same velocity that my body is about to demonstrate on its way to the bottom of Swallow Canyon.

What I need is someone or something to distract her long enough for me to reach that rock protrusion, anchor in, and therefore protect her as well as myself. My goal is to fasten a carabiner to the wall and clip it to the rope between us. Her pull may dislodge her if she loses her footing, but she'd pendulum on my piece of protection after a twenty-five-foot fall, with minimal risk of injury.

I look back at Dominik, whose body language implies he's trying to decide between jumping the falls into the stream (which could easily kill him) and free-climbing down the falls' left side to try to stop Brigit. Either move will force her to act, I'm certain. I shake my head at him, trying to communicate that he should sit tight.

"Three more minutes," Brigit screams gleefully, like she's timing a fun race.

Embrace calm. I squint at the rock knob, picture where the webbing rests inside my pack, and calculate exactly how long it will take to retrieve it and put it to work. I look toward the orange pack on the bush and suddenly know what to do.

"Dad," I shout toward the bush. "Dad, I know where you are, and I know you've planted the backpack there to lure me up. You can see Brigit doesn't want me to have it. And I don't want it. I think she'll leave both of us alone if you take it off the bush and toss it into the stream. Slowly — very, very slowly — so you don't fall."

From an angle that Brigit can't see but Dean can, I tap my harness and point at where my intended anchor sits in the pack. *Understand what I'm really asking, Dean, please. You're a sharp climber, the one and only Mini Spider-Man. If you distract her, I can reach that anchor point before she jerks on the rope. No need to show yourself. Just reach out and dump the pack.*

"You're not tricking me," declares Brigit, but her slightly higher-pitched voice offers me a glimmer of hope. "Two minutes now, if your dad doesn't show."

"Dad, dump the pack!" I order, my voice gone hoarse. "Slow and easy." I creep forward as I speak.

"Sixty seconds, fifty-nine, fifty-eight —" Brigit counts. Her eyes can't be on her watch, me, and the bush all at the same time.

Slowly I move my hand to my backpack buckle while sneaking another foot toward the rocky point.

Well ahead, a hand appears from behind the bush and moves impossibly slowly toward the pack.

"Thanks, Dad," I shout loudly enough to grab Brigit's attention, trembling as I take two more halting steps.

The counting has stopped; no doubt Brigit's mouth is hanging open. But I know better than to look back to see. Her eyes must remain riveted on Dean's hand, because one glance at me and the tug will happen.

"Julian Gordon!" she screams suddenly, and I feel the rope along which my carabiner is moving swing slightly as she moves about on the ledge. "I knew you were down here! I knew you were following us! I don't know how you got yourself and your backpack up there, but — but come out from behind that bush or I'll pull Tristan off his traverse."

"Don't come out till you toss the backpack, Dad," I counter. "Then you can show yourself to Brigit."

"You killed my mother!" Brigit shrieks. "You took her away from us!"

I watch Dean's arm tremble, but to his credit, not withdraw. It continues its painstaking journey toward the backpack; I continue mine to the rock nose.

Three more steps. Two more steps. *Please don't jerk the rope.* One. My hand reaches for the buckle on my pack. The click sounds loud enough to echo through the entire canyon, but only in my imagination. Brigit continues ranting at "my father." Dean's hand has reached the backpack, and he's wriggling it like he's trying to get it off the bush. *Good man, Dean. Keep distracting your sister.*

I produce a nut and wedge it in a crack above the nose of rock. Quickly, I reposition my sling and anchor in. Then I fasten a carabiner to the new safety set-up and clip it to the rope behind me. The second I do so, my father's bag drops to the water, where the current picks it up and drags it downstream, likely never to be seen again. At the same time, Dean uncrouches from behind the bush.

"Brigit," he calls out in a trembling voice. "Please don't hurt Tristan. Or yourself. You're not anchored in right."

I swing around in time to see Brigit's shocked expression, and Dominik completing a daring down-climb, then a sprint up to her ledge behind her.

With an enraged scream, Brigit yanks the rope, and Dominik's hands close around air as she tumbles toward the creek.

CHAPTER 21

We're gathered in the grotto four days later, most of us sitting on camping chairs that Uncle Ted and I hauled out earlier. Mom and Elspeth have installed vanilla-scented candles in each of the grotto's crevices, and Dean has had a fine time lighting them all.

Everyone but Brigit is here: Uncle Ted sitting awkwardly in his low-slung chair; Alex and Elspeth cross-legged beside each another on cushions in the corner; Mom rosy-cheeked and alert; Dominik hunched a bit glumly in his chair; Dean running his eyes around the cavities on the wall; and me in the middle, relating the tale.

Everyone is here except Brigit and Dad, but ever since I read his letter out loud, even Dad seems to be present.

"And then what happened?" asks Mom, leaning forward intently.

"Then Dominik scrambled down and rescued Brigit from where she was swinging with her boots just touching the creek. He unhooked her and calmed her down while I traversed to Dean and set another anchor so he could rappel safely to the ground."

"Could've free-climbed down by myself," Dean insists.

"Not safely," I say soberly.

"And all that time, I was freaking out as I wandered through the woods looking and calling for him," Elspeth says, fidgeting with a large vacuum flask in her lap.

Alex speaks up. "This was all my fault."

Everyone swings around to look at him.

"How do you figure that?" I ask.

"I found the orange backpack during the Search and Rescue expedition, jammed between logs just below Twin Falls. Should have turned it in, but I felt something really heavy in it, so I unbuckled it. I was pretty surprised to find a gold pan inside. I knew instantly then what Julian had been up to in the canyon and wondered if maybe he'd struck it lucky before he drowned. I'd spent most of my days off for years secretly looking for gold in the canyon.

"So I buried the gold pan and rifled through the bag for notes or a map, but panicked when I heard other crew members approaching. I didn't want to turn in the pack in case I'd missed what I was looking for. But I couldn't fit the whole pack into my backpack either. So I tossed out the sleeping bag and some of his clothes, then jammed the bag into my pack."

"Brigit told me she found the boot half-buried in mud beside Twin Falls and the bandana just below that log-jam," Dominik speaks up. "She didn't know Alex had found the pack. She kept the bandana and boot, hid them in her house, and took them with her on the trip last week. She asked me to plant the bandana in that rock tube we went through. The one Tristan calls the airplane. Then, after Tristan found it, she dug it out of his pack and tossed it back in the stream when he wasn't looking. Just to be mean." He hangs his head as if representing her shame.

"Why did you agree to plant the bandana for her?" I ask Dominik.

He sighs. "She convinced me it would help you and your mom, and I did not see any harm in it. I was so into her I would have done almost anything for her then, to be honest."

We wait as he goes silent for a moment.

"I did not know she had the boot," he says. "I did not know she was planting boot prints for you." He hangs his head.

Unlike my mom, who has been released from the hospital, Brigit is in the mental health ward of the nearby hospital for treatment. She has also undergone interrogation by the police for attempted murder. Meanwhile, some aunt of theirs no one but Brigit knew about has arrived in town to look after Dean.

Alex resumes his story. "When I got home from the search for Julian, I went through that orange pack again, found nothing, and felt really guilty. I hid it in the back of my workshop, meaning to return it to the canyon someday. But I was as afraid of getting caught returning it as I was of having disobeyed Search and Rescue rules in the first place."

"I found it while cleaning his workshop last week," Elspeth says, picking up the tale. "It was marked with Julian's name, and I guessed how it had gotten there. It was after you three had left on your trip already, so I couldn't give it to Tristan. And I didn't want to give it to Mary; I wanted Tristan to give it to Mary.

"I didn't dare ask Alex about it, because I remembered he was on the Search and Rescue mission for Julian, and I knew he shouldn't have it. I didn't want him mad at me for questioning him, and I didn't want to get him in trouble by telling anyone else. Plus, I kept thinking about Tristan trying so hard to find something of his dad's in the canyon at that very moment. I asked Dean what he thought of us getting ahead of your party and planting it. That way, Tristan could give it to his mother, and it might help her get better. He said it was a stupid idea. But then he disappeared on me with the pack. It's my fault for giving him the idea and not locking him in his room, I guess." She does her best to glare at her babysitting charge, but Dean just returns a weak smirk.

"But I was already better by then," Mom inserts, patting Elspeth's knee. "When Tristan left to do the Lower Canyon, I was terrified he wouldn't come back. I had a panic attack. Uncle Ted took me to the hospital, and they got me turned around. I still feel terrible about all the trouble I caused by not facing up to Julian's death, and suspecting — well, the letter put us all straight, didn't it?"

"It was me who got Tristan onto the Upper Canyon day trip for free," Alex says, "with some help from Brigit and Elspeth."

"And me," Dean says.

"But only because I suggested it," Elspeth prompts Alex. "I could tell that poor Tristan needed some outdoors time away from home, and I believed he'd find something of his father's. Blame it on my extrasensory perception if you want, but we wouldn't have Julian's letter otherwise."

"Where would we be without your ESP, honey?" Alex teases Elspeth, nudging her. "Anyway, so I did a hike along the rim that day to observe Tristan and make sure his skills were up to the Lower Canyon, since my guide Brigit was so insistent on taking him there. And having known Brigit for years — I canyoneered with her when I travelled up to the Lillooet area long before she moved here — I never in a million years suspected she had mental health issues."

"She did not have problems then," Dominik speaks up. "It was only recently she went off her medications. And she asked me to tell all of you that she is very, very sorry. That she should not have believed her mom and Tristan's dad were messing around. And she should not have set up this trip."

"No, she shouldn't have," I say firmly, then scan the gathering. "Who here kicked over a pile of rocks the day Dominik and I were out tracking?"

"I did not know it at the time, but Brigit was following us," Dominik says. He sighs and lowers his voice. "She hated you, but she was not herself."

"And Dean," I continue, "when you told me my mom hadn't told me everything, you meant that you believed my dad and your mom had run off together?"

"Uh-huh," he says, frowning and wriggling in his chair.

"I want everyone to know I will be talking to Search and Rescue tomorrow," Alex says. "I will come clean about not having turned in Julian's pack. I deserve whatever they do to me about that."

I nod at him approvingly. My respect for him just went up.

Uncle Ted finally speaks. "So, what about the gold? You had a meeting about it yesterday, Mary. What gives?"

"We've formally registered a claim," Mary replies, smiling. "So the site is ready for panning. We'll be hiring a professional to help with that. If we make money, a percentage will go into a trust fund for Dean, and to Brigit. In the meantime, I'll be returning to work at the bakery."

"Lucky sods," Alex says, smiling. "All those days I spent looking for a gold vein. Never found anything."

"My bakery earnings, plus the possibility of a share of gold profits, hopefully mean our family won't have to close down or sell the store," Mom continues.

"Thank goodness!" says Uncle Ted, squeezing my shoulder.

"Sorry about that, Alex," Mom says, "but we appreciate your willingness to serve as general manager until Tristan is out of school."

"After graduation, maybe we can do a deal." I wink at Alex. "You do the canyon trips, and I do the retail stuff. We can swap off whenever we get bored."

"Bored? Nothing to do with Swallow Canyon or canyoneering is ever boring!" says Alex.

"Certainly sounds like this last trip wasn't," Mom says soberly. "But just to remind you, we're gathered here today to honour —" She chokes up.

"— Julian," Uncle Ted finishes.

"And acknowledge his death," Mom says, bravely. "And the death of Evelyn Dowling, who, like Julian, was only trying to improve her family's financial situation."

"Ahem," says Elspeth, a pleased smile on her face. "I've got a flask of organic lavender herbal tea and some mugs here." She leans down to pick up a tray of cups and begins pouring and passing them around.

"And I've baked a cake," Mom announces.

She lifts the cover of a glass cake stand I haven't seen her use in months. My mouth waters to glimpse rich-looking chocolate and vanilla icing forming some kind of design on the top. We all move in for a closer look. It's a swallow with wings spread from one tip of the cake to another, representing Swallow Canyon.

"Made with love in memory of Julian and Evelyn," Mom says.

I give her a peck on the cheek.

CHAPTER 22

Early the next morning, I sneak out of my bedroom before dawn. As I glide noiselessly past my mother's room, I peer in. She looks up from where she's reading, smiles, and holds out her hand.

"Going tracking? Good for you," she says, her face a healthy pink in the glow of her bedside lamp as I step in, and we squeeze hands over her freshly washed quilt. "Take your time. Enjoy yourself."

"I will," I say.

I skip down the worn stair treads and detect a lemon scent in the kitchen as my bare feet pad over the shiny-clean floor. It's all Mom's doing, along with a tin of strawberry muffins fresh-baked last evening. I grab one to take along.

A gentle push and the back door flies open without a squeak. I'm soon jogging along the forest floor, my heart singing with the birds, my spirits rising with the sun.

I feel Dad with me. We always tracked together, so this is our time of day. We spot some deer tracks and veer off the trail after them, slowing, consumed by the joy of being outdoors, the thrill and anticipation of following a wild creature.

I slow down, clear my mind, and make myself invisible. A breeze stirs the trees, and an eagle swoops high above.

Soon I'm within sight of a mother deer and her only fawn. *Is the fawn the same one that lost its smaller sibling?* If so, it's already larger, more alert and capable-looking than the last time I saw it. Perhaps the trauma has woven itself seamlessly into its life experience. It is losing its spots; soon it will be independent of its vigilant mother.

I watch a while, then carry on to the canyon rim. I pause there and breathe deeply, letting all my senses draw in the calming smells and sounds of the forest around me before pulling the dented blue aluminum water bottle from my pack.

Lifting it high, I toast Dad's legacy to me. The ability to track and canyoneer, without which I would not have survived the Lower Canyon trip, nor found what he left for me. The sixteen years of love that enables me to forgive Brigit, as he would have wanted. The determination to join forces with Mom, so we can carry on. And a love of nature.

I scan left, right, and down. Below, the creek tumbles effortlessly over obstacles, oblivious of time. Of course, I don't forget to look up. There, as the swallows soar in exhilarating circles, I feel Dad put his hands gently on my shoulders and squeeze them like he's proud of me — of who I am and whomever I may choose to become.

ACKNOWLEDGEMENTS

Above all, I'd like to acknowledge Dominik Nadolski, a long-time California canyoneer who helped with both early-stage plotting and technical details of the sport, and who patiently read several drafts in between our Skype conversations. He even sent me occasional YouTube links to help me understand this relatively new and technical sport I was writing about. His passion for canyoneering (also called canyoning) was definitely infectious.

My other canyoneering guide was Francois-Xavier de Ruydts, whose photography of the sport in Mountain Life magazine's Summer 2013 edition (www.mountainlifemedia.ca) was the novel's original spark. Check out his award-winning short film of exploring canyons near Squamish, British Columbia, Canada (where this novel is set): "Down the Line" (https://vimeo.com/64671839). Francois-Xavier was kind enough to meet up, show me gear, and later read over the manuscript. The novel is dedicated to his infant daughter who arrived during the process.

The talented Allyson Latta was invaluable and a delight to work with, and a shout-out to Colin Thomas, as well. As always, a hug to my friend Silvana Bevilacqua, who puts up with long discussions of my characters as they evolve. And to my ever-encouraging husband, Steve, who never gets to see my writing until it's about to be submitted, and always offers astute remarks at that point. I also appreciated geological input offered by the late Rolf Kellerhals.

My new teen editor, Vansh Bali, gave very perceptive feedback and knew which cover option he liked best. And although I always thank my agent, Lynn Bennett, this time she really went above and beyond. Thanks for your patience, persistence, feedback, and loyalty, Lynn.

For background research, I'd like to credit *Canyoneering* by Christopher Van Tilburg and books by tracker Tom Brown Jr. (www.trackerschool.com).

Finally, thanks to Dundurn Press for taking on the story, in particular Kirk Howard, Margaret Bryant, Carrie Gleason, Cheryl Hawley, Jaclyn Hodsdon, Kathryn Lane, Jennifer Mannering, and Jenny McWha — but all the team, for sure!

OF RELATED INTEREST

The Merit Birds
Kelley Powell

2015 Dewey Divas Pick
2016 Booklist Top Ten Multicultural Fiction
List, Youth Spotlight

Cam is finally settling into his new life in Laos when tragedy strikes and he's wrongfully accused of murder.

Eighteen-year-old Cam Scott is angry. He's angry about his absent dad, he's angry about being angry, and he's angry that he has had to give up his Ottawa basketball team to follow his mom to her new job in Vientiane, Laos. However, Cam's anger begins to melt under the Southeast Asian sun as he finds friendship with his neighbour, Somchai, and gradually falls in love with Nok, who teaches him about building merit, or karma, by doing good deeds, such as purchasing caged "merit birds."

Tragedy strikes and Cam finds himself falsely accused of a crime. His freedom depends on a person he's never met. A person who knows that the only way to restore his merit is to confess. *The Merit Birds* blends action, suspense, and humour in a far-off land where things seem so different, yet deep down are so much the same.

And Then the Sky Exploded
David A. Poulsen

When Christian learns his great-grandfather helped build the A-bombs dropped on Japan, he wants to make amends … somehow.

While attending the funeral of his great-grandfather, ninth-grader Christian Larkin learns that the man he loved and respected was a member of the Manhattan Project, the team that designed and created the atomic bombs dropped on Japan during the Second World War.

On a school trip to Japan, Chris meets eighty-one-year-old Yuko, who was eleven when the first bomb exploded over Hiroshima, horribly injuring her. Christian is determined to do something to make up for what his great-grandfather did. But after all this time, what can one teenager really do? His friends tell him it's a stupid idea, that there's nothing he can do. And maybe they're right.

But maybe, just maybe … they're wrong.

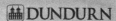